The

Bellus

Prophecy

Leon Michaels

1

Books by Leon Michaels

The Path Home

From the Mists of Darkness

Task Force Nemesis

Tales From The Bench

The Echelon Factor

The Morbius Expedition

Three Against The Darkness

Random Acts Of Science Fiction

Willem

Today is Yesterday's Tomorrow

"The Denoyelles Family Saga"

The Hanover Throne

The Bellus Project

The Bellus Legacy

The Bellus Myth

The Bellus Solution

The Bellus Prophecy

"The Crane Equation Trilogy"

The Crane Equation: The Early Years

The Crane Equation: Rebuilding a Nation

The Crane Equation: The Crane Legacy

"The Black Ops Series"

Operation Damocles

Operation Dokkaebi

Operation Yofune-Nushi

Operation Kartikeya

The Black Orchid

The Twenty-First Special Operations Group: Book One: Family

The Twenty-First Special Operations Group: Book Two: Operators

Operation Heracles

Operation Pandora

Acknowledgments

To My Wife for tolerating my bothering her to read and edit my manuscripts.

To the young man who read the Bellus Project and asked when a sequel would be coming out. This is the fourth sequel to that book and hopefully, the last.

Note: I find pictures on the internet which have no credit or copywrite notices on them to use for covers. I do hope I have not infringed on anyone's rights as I utilize those pictures for my covers.

This is a work of Fiction. Any similarities to individuals past or present is unintentional and purely a coincidence. Any similarities to any individual in the future is pure Karma.

Earth Date 7193

The President of the Hayutan Federation stepped up to the podium in front of a joint meeting of the Parliament. The chamber was full as all attending were awaiting the news which the President was to present to them. A hush came over the chamber as he prepared to speak.

"Ladies and Gentlemen. I have received word through Her Royal Highness, Princess Lujayn, that we have an heir to the Throne of Hayuta. His Highness, Prince Alexander has sired an heir to the Throne by his wife, Consuela."

"Princess Lujayn gave no further information concerning the sex of the child, only that the silver hair was present. Princess Lujayn did state that the child's hair was not fully silver but did have a wide silver streak from its forehead to the back of its head while the rest of the child's hair was as she described it, fiery red like the child's mother."

"I put it to the members of Parliament. The requirement for the hair of silver has never stated part or all. Only that the ruler has that trait. I put it to the members of Parliament to vote yea to accept this child as heir to the Throne, or nay, to stay the fulfilling of the Throne until a child is born a complete head of silver hair."

"Vote now please."

Each member of Parliament carried a baton approximately one hundred and sixty millimeters in length with buttons on both ends. One end was painted green for Yea, the other red for Nay.

Once pressed, the tally of votes would show on a large screen behind the podium.

The President turned to view the screen as the votes were tallied. Three hundred and forty-seven voted Yea. Thirty-six voted Nay. Once the vote was set, the President posted his vote. Yea.

He turned back to the audience, struck a gavel three times.

"Members of Parliament, the vote has been taken and sealed. We have an heir to the Throne. I will transmit the results to Her Highness, Princess Lujayn so she can advise Prince Alexander of our decision. May the Saints watch over Hayuta."

Ten minutes later, the leaders of the various political parties were standing in the President's office as he sent the message to Princess Lujayn. The de facto leader of Parliament waited until the message was sent before speaking.

"Robbie, it's alright that we have an heir, but where is the child? No one knows where Prince Alexander is even located. What planet he and his family are even on? If needed, how do we contact Prince Alexander since he is now regent to the Throne until the child comes of age?"

"Samuel, you sat in chambers when Prince Alexander renounced the Throne. Even now, nearly ten years later I can still hear his voice as he spoke of what he would do if he was called to return to the Throne. All we can do is govern as Princess Lujayn laid down in the Principles of Leadership when she turned over the Worlds to the people. We must abide by those Principles. It is the people that wish to see the Throne occupied and they have been peaceful, knowing that Prince Alexander is out amongst the universe if needed, and now we can tell them he has an heir."

He looked at the men and one woman in his office.

"If we fail to abide by the Principles of Leadership, then the people will demand that the Throne is occupied. I suggest each of us go back and study the Principles and remember what our function and purpose is within these chambers, so we do not give the people a position from which to demand our removal."

Seventeen Years Later

Jilena Kaylani Donovan was the twelfth child of the Forge Master of Hollis, Michael Donovan. What set her apart from her siblings was her red hair and the three-centimeter strip of silver hair that ran from over her right eye down the back of her head. Unlike her sisters, who averaged one point five meters in height, she stood one point eight and only had two brothers that stood taller. Her fiery red hair and bright blue eyes came from her mother, but her height she inherited from her father as she also inherited the silver hair.

To the universe, Michael Donovan was the Forge Master who lived outside of the city of Brentwood, on the world named Hollis after its discoverer. His work was in blades, swords and knives, but would work any manner of steel, needing made or repaired. Anyone visiting his forge would say his over the shoulder long hair and his neatly trimmed beard and mustache was grey, but that was due to the ash from the forge concealing his bright, silver hair. Hair that belonged to his real name, Alexander Mikhail LaSalle Borland, Prince of Hayuta, Bellus and Protector of Keres.

Jilena was slender, weighting just a few grams over seventy-seven kilos which was deceptive since her body showed the definition of a person who spent hours developing muscle instead of the softness most young women lived with. This came from having a Centaurian mother and two Centaurian step-mothers, all who had been mercenaries. Mercenaries of the Free Lance Infantry who stood alongside the Marines of the Federation Fleet who kept peace within the Federation.

All of Michael Donovan's children worked in his forge at one time or another, learning the secrets of molding steel into the desired form and function. Except at the age Jilena's sisters left the forge to learn more gentle aspects of their sex, Jilena stayed in the forge and learned how to craft blades under her father's tutelage.

This was not to say Jilena had not learned the same lessons and skills her sisters did away from the forge, but her body was firmer, stronger as she grew older.

Today was her seventeenth birthday, a day she had been dreading for some time as she would soon leave for Bellus and enter the university as all of her elder siblings had done. Also, as with her siblings, she was home schooled and had scored high in her placement exams for the university, especially the engineering aspects of the exams.

As Jilena dried herself off from her shower, she looked at her body in the floor to ceiling mirror of her room. Except for being kissed a few times by one of the apprentices in her father's forge, she was untouched, unknown to boy or man. Her mother and step-mothers had gone to great lengths explaining the facts of life to her as they had done with all of her elder sisters, but Jilena knew there had to be more than that, especially considering her father kept three wives content. But the Master's bedroom was isolated from the rest of the house and it was forbidden to enter into the passageway to it once the doors were closed.

Her mother and step-mothers had separate bedrooms, but none of the children ever knew if he had one or all three wives in his large bed on any given night.

Jilena dressed modestly for the small party in her honor, wearing a light green dress which only gave a hint to her breasts, yet accented her slim hips as it fell just short of her ankles. The dress was slit in four places up above her knees, showing a modest amount of thigh when she set down. Her only jewelry were small diamond studs for her ears and her freckled, yet creamy complexion had no need to makeup, even on her full lips.

Tonight, she had special guests. Her father's parents had arrived along with her mother's uncle, Ismael by a shuttle which sat on the pad behind the house. The shuttle which would take her away from her home and family to her grandparent's yacht, the Areta.

Her mother came for her to advise her it was time to greet her guests.

"Jilena, everyone is waiting for you. Please, come and enjoy the party."

"Mother, do I have to leave? I mean go to Bellus?"

"No dear. By the laws of Hollis, you have reached your majority. But until you go out into the universe, you cannot properly be prepared for it. We have discussed this in length over the past year. You have a special place in the universe and you must prepare for it."

"Yes Mother, a special place. As much as I like the blend on my hair, it is a curse upon this family. And because of the curse, I must hide my heritage until I can complete the university. Dye my hair so no one will know who I really am."

"I know it is all too confusing Jilena. To have two separate identities. I shed my fur, my Centaurian heritage to hid amongst normal humans so the love of my life, your father could have some measure of peace. Each day he covers his hair with ash to hide who he is. The universe lays burdens upon all of us which we must either defeat or give into. I fought the burden of loving your father till it nearly killed me, then I awoke to realize once I surrendered to it, my life was complete. You are still young, enjoy life as much as you can, while you can."

"Thank you, mother. Now I guess it is time for me to face my future."

The Northern Rim

Jilena exited her sanitary facilities, drying herself off from her shower after removing the sweat and smell of her lover who was still on her bed. She had turned twenty-five the month before and her body was still as firm as it was at seventeen. She took her father's advice about lovers to heart in that she only took one at a time while on a cruise or deployed to a new planet, building a base of operations.

She was a Fleet Construction Engineer at the rank of Lieutenant Commander, overseeing the building of a new Fleet Outpost on the world known as Dagur. This lover was a Centaurian, a Fleet Master Chief who handled the explosives for this assignment. Jilena looked at him thinking maybe another go at destroying the sheets before duty, but then she would have to shower again. It wasn't that he was well endowed, because he was about average, but she did love the feeling of his soft fur against her as they made love.

"Off your ass Morgan, time to get to work." She spoke as she threw her damp towel at him.

He grumbled as he tossed the towel back at her.

"Damn woman, you work a man to death during the day, then try to kill him in your bed at night. But I'd give a year's pay for a night with you and hope the medics can revive me later."

"I haven't killed you yet, so stop your gripping. Besides, there is nothing requiring you to return to my bed, is there?"

"Yes, there is. I would hate to think you crippled one of the men because I wasn't in your bed."

Jilena laughed as he crawled out of bed and stood in front of her. She wrapped her arms around his neck and kissed him before responding to his comment.

13

"Go get cleaned up Master Chief, we have work to be done."

She was dressed by the time he came out of the shower and again she wished there was time for more fun, but as she had told him, there was work to be done.

"Jilena I have meant to ask you. Why do you have hair dye for a woman your age?"

"It's because I am cursed. My hair started turning premature gray even before I started the university. My father has the same problem but at his age now, he has no concern for his looks, but I am vain."

"Padron my asking. So, do you want the Northeast corner blown out this morning?"

The work progressed according to schedule even with a few glitches in the planning. Buildings went up and soon there was a second company of Marines brought in to assist in protecting the site. When there was no more need for an explosives expert on site, Morgan, Jilena's lover was shipped off to another project half-way across the known universe. Jilena waited a month before taking another lover, this time one of the Marine company commanders. This was almost her undoing.

Boris Everard was a Hayutan who had joined the Fleet Marines. What started as a one night of enjoyment for Jilena carried through for several weeks until he commented on her silver roots of her hair which was needing dyed. He continued to address her roots as silver until she became angry with him and tossed him out of her bed, telling him she knew of the Bellus Legend since she had gone to the university there and did not wish to hear another word about it, even a rumor of it.

That evening she contacted her father via the Hayutan Communication Crystal she carried and told him what had happened. Two days later, Boris had orders to a staff assignment on the other side of the known universe. Jilena swore she would never take another Hayutan lover regardless of how long she had to stay celibate.

The base was completed on schedule and Jilena had the pleasure of turning over command of the facility to her older brother, Mikhail Donovan, who was a full Commander in the Fleet.

Her next assignment was to survey and set a design for a new base a thousand parsecs from the quarantined planet Xylia, where her parents had met. This planet had not yet been named.

Planet RL-66941

Jilena made planet fall with a company of Marines who would act as security and also help her survey the locations best suited for a base. One main factor was a steady supply of fresh water. Ocean or salt water could be refined to fresh water but that was another step in the process the Fleet tried to avoid. Over the past decades, the Federation Congress was tightening the belts of the Fleet, trying to save every Krone they could, especially in building new bases for exploration and Federation protection.

She spent her days doing the survey and her nights laying it out on paper, defining what would need to be done and the equipment to do it with. Jilena had a pre-fab office and living quarters for this assignment while her Marines were living as many Marines do, on the ground in tents. But they did have a pre-fab kitchen on location and the Marines had a shower point to clean themselves at nightly.

Three weeks into the survey, the Frigate Bonny, which had been watching over the survey received a call to assist a disabled freighter on the edge of known space. She boosted, leaving two Scout ships to provide support and cover. Four days later, one of the Scout ships reported the Bonny returning with four unknown ships according to the Fleet IFF recorder. The fact the other ships were not transmitting IFF signals worried Jilena and the Scout ship Captains.

Jilena ordered the Marines to gear up for battle and disperse, making it harder for them to zero in on a large target from space. She quickly changed into a Marine uniform, complete with everything a Marine would carry plus the set of swords her father made for her when she was twelve. She also had three knives she had forged on her body along with her sub-carbine and pistol. She filled the two-liter water bladder in her survival pack, put her communications crystal in reach and activated it. Her mother responded in seconds.

"What's up Jilena?" Her mother asked.

"Mom, we have unknown ships entering the system and the Frigate Bonny was dispatched to assist a disabled freighter. We are preparing to disperse into the jungle if the ships prove to be Raiders."

"I'll contact your grandmother and let her know you may be in trouble there. Stay calm and work the situation as best you can."

"I will Mom, thanks."

Twenty minutes later, the Scout ship Keijser reported missile launches from the approaching ships. Jilena ordered the Marines to disperse as she opened the channel to her mother.

"Mom I only have seconds here. The approaching ships have opened fire on our covering Scout ships. We are dispersing, I'll contact you when I can."

Jilena did not wait for a response as she shut off the crystal, then put in her pack as she headed for the door of her quarters. Outside, she was greeted by a team of Marines and together, they headed into the jungle away from the camp. As she moved deeper and deeper into the jungle. She was getting reports first from the Scout ships, then other Marines on the ground. Both Scout ships were destroyed in nearly an hour-long battle scoring hits on the Raider ships.

She had two thoughts as they worked their way into the thick undergrowth. First, somehow the Raiders has ghosted or cloned the IFF signal of the Bonny. Second, there was nothing to gain by hitting this camp as they had nothing of real value other than the weapons they carried, unless the Raiders had a base in a nearby system and this base would threaten theirs.

One good thought in her mind was that even if the Raiders had blocked any alerts sent by the Scouts, her Mother would already have talked to Grandmother Lujayn, who would be sending dozens of ships in her direction. Grandmother Lujayn may not sit upon the Throne of Hayuta, but no one on Hayuta, or within the Fleet would hesitate in following her orders to send ships to Planet RL-66941.

They had been moving for over two hours when Jilena called for a break. The Marines spread out and she motioned to the team leader she was stepping out to relieve her bladder. She had just finished her business and was pulling up her pants when a shuttle passed over their position and dropped a charge through the heavy canopy, exploding about a meter off the ground.

The concussion from the explosion threw her several meters further away from the Marines. She picked herself up and shook the effects of the blast off the best she could. If she had taken her helmet off, or even had raised the face shield, she would have been deafened by the blast. She staggered to where her pack and swords were lying, picked them up and went to see how much damage the bomb had done.

In her helmet she heard a jumble of signals from Marines reporting being bombed by shuttles. She instructed her helmet AI to go cold which caused her face shield to go clear as she entered the location where her Marines had been. Four were dead, their bodies mangled. The fifth was alive but had a large tree branch through his body. He died as she tried to help him.

Jilena dumped the packs of the Marines and shoved the rations they carried into one pack along with ammunition before she took off at a jog further into the jungle. Just before dark, she took her helmet off and listened for any sounds that might tell her of trouble. She instructed her helmet to use minimal power and listen only for radio traffic. She heard nothing by static. Jilena found a place to hunker down, ate a ration, then covered herself with her poncho and went to sleep.

18

She was awakened by a beeping sound realizing her crystal had been activated from the sender's end. Jilena dug the crystal out of her pack, sat it on the ground as she stayed covered up and activated her end. She figured it was her mother, instead she had her grandmother on the other end.

"Jilena, what is your status?"

"Grandmother, I'm alive only by the grace of the Saints and my bladder. I stepped away from my Marine escort to relieve myself and a shuttle dropped a bomb in the middle of my escorts, killing all five of them. I was shook up, but uninjured."

"Yes, bless the Saints for that. Every ship along the rim is heading your way, some are cutting across unknown space to get to you. Do you have any idea the status of your Marines?"

"Grandmother I'm sure you know, both Scout ships have been destroyed, and if my team was killed, I can only imagine that most of the company has been decimated. I think they have somehow found a way to track our comm links, our AI's in our helmets are constantly talking to each other and whomever it is attacking us has queued in on that."

"Yes Jilena, that sounds plausible, especially if they have found a way to clone our IFF signals. You'll have no more contact with myself or your parents until we have the situation under control over the planet. Find a place to hole up and go to ground. Remember your survival training and the lessons you learned on your mother's lap. They will serve you well. All of the family are praying to the Saints for your safe return."

"Thank you, Grandmother."

Jilena broke the connection thinking her grandmother looked older, worn. She put the crystal back in her pack, checked her chronometer, then curled back up and went back to sleep with her pistol in her hand.

She walked for two more days utilizing the compass in her vest to maintain a straight line away from the camp site as she searched for a place to provide her with some shelter until relief could get to her. It was late in the day when she came to a bluff with a small stream running along in front of it. Jilena looked at the ground carefully, looking for any sign of animal or human traffic. The ground was virgin, nothing had crossed in this area for several weeks, since the last rain.

Jilena checked the water to find it was near pure and using her water filters, refilled her nearly empty water bladder. She was thankful it was cool under the canopy otherwise her water may not have lasted as long as it did. The water was warm enough that she stripped off her uniform and took a bath in the stream after wearing her uniform for three days straight. In her pack was a lightweight set of coveralls so she put them on and washed her uniform then laid it over bushes to dry.

From the bottom of her pack she took a tightly rolled up screening web. She anchored it against the bluff, ran it out to a tree then back to the bluff again. Jilena then went back around the screen, anchoring it to the ground with twigs and whatever she could come up with. Once she was happy with her screen, she moved her drying uniforms inside the screen and just hooked them on the inside of the screen to dry and away from any animal that might think they were something to enjoy.

She took the Marine issue entrenching tool off her pack and began scrapping out a sleeping pad, leveling the ground and tossing any rocks she found out of the way. Next, she dug a small pit with air flow notches, so she could heat water for tea. The rations were self-heating, but the tea was not.

It was dark by the time she had accomplished this plus gathering a small bunch of twigs to use for a fire in the morning. She just sat, leaning back against the rocky surface of the bluff, thinking about what she had to do next. To her it was simple. Find a source of food to supplement her rations.

A normal survival pack contained a week's worth of high energy rations at two rations a day, she had gathered at least three more weeks from the dead Marines, but it would take a minimum of a week for relief to get to her if any capital ships were close enough. Ships large enough to tackle the Raiders if they were still in orbit. But she had not heard a single shuttle making an over flight for days.

The next morning, she fixed a cup of hot tea to go with her morning rations. Her uniform was still damp, so she left it hanging to dry more along with her underwear. She rearranged her pack, filling it with the rations from the pack she took from the Marines, then laid out what she had left over to eat while in her shelter. The pack was set up now in case she had to abandon her shelter.

Suddenly Jilena found herself with nothing to do but wait for relief. She considered utilizing her helmet's AI to study the Survival Manual contained in it. But she was concerned that the Raiders might be able to home in on the AI's signal. She just laid down and tried to relax the best she could.

Just after midday, she checked her uniform and dressed for a fight if one came her way. She hated the Plastron Armor, but it would protect her vital organs from small arms fire.

She bathed every other day to maintain sanitary conditions the best she could, washing her hair every other time to insure it was clean and bug free. What she did not realize was the nature of the water. It was free of contaminates and safe to drink, but it slowly washed the red dye from her silver hair.

On the fourth day she decided to venture out and see if she could find some berries to enjoy with her evening rations, maybe even boil some down and make a fruit drink.

Jilena was picking some red berries that they had in the survey camp site that had been tested and found flavorful. She tried to keep one eye on her surroundings as she picked the berries, but she found herself suddenly in a bad situation.

She found herself looking at a Liger crouched within five meters from her. Ligers were what appeared to be a cross between an Earth Lion and a Tiger, with their primary fangs being on the average of one hundred millimeters long. She slowly shifted her stance as she watched the animal. There was no way she could draw her pistol to defend herself, but she was wearing both her swords. Drawing her long sword in the manner of countering an attack on her seemed like the logical tactic if the Liger attacked her.

The animal jumped at her with its claws extended and mouth open, ready to sink its fangs into her. She side-stepped as she dropped the berries and grabbed her sword, pulling and sweeping upward with it as the animal went by her. She felt the blade connect with the animal as one paw reached out, raking its claws across her left leg. She screamed as the pain of the claws tearing at the flesh of her leg but rotated to meet the return attack of the animal.

But the Liger did not turn to attack her a second time. Her blade had swept up under the neck of the animal and nearly severed its head from its body. Jilena hobbled to the animal and with a downward cut, finished removing the head from the beast, then leaned back against the nearest tree so she could examine the wounds to her leg.

The claw marks were not as deep as she expected after she cut her pants open. Jilena pulled an antiseptic spray from her vest and sprayed the wounds feeling the sting of the antiseptic then watch as it sealed the wounds, stopping the blood flow down her leg. Carefully she worked a dressing inside her torn pants around the wound then clipped the tear in her pants before standing up.

Jilena walked around a bit to see if the leg was going to tolerate the movement then looked at the Liger. No one would believe her story about defeating a Liger with just a blade, even if it was a long sword. But if she had the fangs, no one could deny her story. Jilena carefully cut the fangs from the Liger's mouth, then decided she wanted the pelt.

She had skinned a variety of animals back on Hollis, so she figured she could deal with the Liger. When she rolled the animal over to make the first cut, she discovered she had killed a female and its nipples were leaking milk meaning she had kittens in the area. Jilena did not try to be neat, only that she did not cut the pelt, so it could be tanned intact without holes in it.

Just as she had the pelt rolled up she heard a soft purring from the other side of the berry patch. She stood as she drew her pistol, so she was ready this time and waited for the next animal to show itself. But when it did, it was a small creature, a Liger kitten that looked as if it was barely born.

Jilena had killed the kittens mother but now the baby would starve without its mother's milk. Her first instinct was to kill the kitten to put it out of its misery of starving to death, but she could not do it. She holstered her pistol, then went to the kitten. It was so young, it was not scared of her as she gently rubbed its head before she picked it up.

She carried the kitten back to her shelter and just sat it down along with the pelt. The kitten went to the pelt and whined, nuzzling the pelt as if looking for a nipple to feed from.

Jilena dug into her survival kit for her main first aid kit and took to antibiotics to counter anything the antiseptic might have missed. Once she had that out of the way, she took the small cook set from her pack and using the bowl, she mixed up some of the dry creamer that came with the rations. It took her a while to introduce the kitten to the mixture by sticking its nose in it until the kitten learned to lick at the mixture. She held the bowl and kitten until it had licked all it wanted the began to worm around in her hand, wanting down.

She took the time to braid a harness for the kitten using cord from her pack making the harness, so it would also go around the neck and behind its front legs. As she was putting the harness on the kitten, she discovered this was a male Liger. Jilena drove a stake into the ground, then tied the lead she had made to it then to the harness. She put the pelt near the kitten, so it would have something to snuggle up to.

Jilena laid down to stretch out her leg and just thought about what had happened to her today. She then remembered she had not cleaned her sword, so she got up and took the sword down to the stream and washed the Liger's blood from the blade. Jilena checked the edge of the blade and had to smile at the fact her father had forged an extremely sharp and durable blade.

Then she thought about the blood, her blood on her uniform and her leg. What if the smell attracted another Liger? She sat down on the stream bank and removed her boots then pants. She had blood down her leg to where her boot top was located. She washed her leg then her pants. There was blood on her boots inside and outside of it. She washed her boot, then walked back to the shelter carrying her pants and boots.

As she sat on her poncho, she sewed up the rips in her pants leg, then hung them up to dry before laying down with her pistol where she could grab it if needed. The sound of the Liger kitten purring put her to sleep.

Every day she fed the kitten after she checked the wound on her leg to check for infection. The kitten began to accept her as she fed it and she even let it run free inside the shelter a few times. It would come to her during those times when hungry. The only time she left the shelter area was to refill her bladder and to wash her eating things.

Eleven days after the raid on the survey camp, her crystal pinged. She set it up and answered the call.

"Jilena, the relief force is entering the system and sensors do not show anyone or anything above the planet. Wait two hours then power up your helmets comm."

"Yes, Grandmother, thank you?"

"Now, how are you doing?"

"I had a bit of a run in with a Liger, but I'm alright."

"Excuse me Jilena? A Liger and you're alright?"

"Yes Grandmother, it managed to get a couple of claws across my left leg, but it lost the argument. I now have its fangs and pelt. Oh, and a kitten to keep me company."

"You have a Liger kitten?"

"Yes Grandmother. It appeared to be newly born and I could not bring myself to kill it. He's been good company, even sleeping with me now."

"Amazing Jilena. So, get ready to be picked up."

"Again, thank you Grandmother. I know you will tell my parents I am doing good, but please express my love to them and to Grandfather. Hopefully I will see them soon."

"I shall Jilena."

"Love you Grandmother."

"Love you too Jilena."

Jilena gathered everything up and made ready to be rescued. She was leaving the screen up since it would take too much time to take back down and it would self-destruct after ninety days. She was fully suited up when she heard the call to her. Jilena responded and told the AI to broadcast a locator signal.

25

Twenty minutes later an armored assault boat hovered near the stream and dropped a penetrator through the canopy for her to ride back up on. Jilena had the kitten inside her vest as best as she could since a Liger kitten is a bit larger than a full-grown house cat.

Inside the assault boat, the Marines assisted in getting her removed from the penetrator and relieved her of her pack. The boat's Corpsman helped her to one of the seats and inquired on her health.

"Commander, we have a report you were injured."

"Yes, about eight or nine days ago. This little furball's mother decided I looked like dinner, but I'm alright now."

Jilena rubbed between the kitten's ears and it loudly purred. The Corpsman looked at the Liger kitten then the pelt tied to her pack and just shook his head.

"We'll have to take you to Medical when we get aboard the Boyington, to make sure the doctor takes a look at the injury."

"Yes, thank you Corpsman."

The boats pilot notified the Frigate Boyington they had Jilena and were lifting to orbit. He also advised the Frigate that a cage would need to be available for a Liger kitten. The Frigate asked for a confirmation on the cage for a Liger kitten and the pilot linked the Corpsman's helmet camera to the comm link and showed the kitten in Jilena's vest.

Onboard the Frigate, she was met by the ship's Captain and Doctor. A small animal containment cage was there for the kitten and one of the Marines on the boat was carrying her pack with the Liger pelt attached. She asked the Captain if she could keep the kitten in her quarters until they made landfall where she could turn it over to an animal welfare center. The Captain was unsure about doing that until she took her helmet off.

26

Jilena was so tired, she did not realize she had boarded a Hayutan Frigate. Her silver streak in her red hair startled everyone in the hanger bay.

"Your Highness, please accept my apologizes for not being aware who you are. You may use my stateroom as your quarters and of course, the kitten can be placed in there with you."

"Your Highness? What are you talking about Captain?"

"Your hair your Highness, your silver hair."

"Oh frack! Captain, I am only a Lieutenant Commander in the Federation Fleet. I only require quarters suitable for a Lieutenant Commander. Please, direct me to such quarters and if possible, a new uniform to I can get cleaned up and get some rest."

"Yes, Your Highness. Right this way please."

She was taken to the medically facility for a physical which was standard practice for castaways. The doctor told her the leg was healing nicely and they could insure there would be no scars from the Liger's claws. Jilena thought about it but this was a battle wound in her book, one no one would believe without seeing the scars. She told him no, to let them heal and she would wear them with pride. After all, how many people could claim to have met a Liger face to face and defeated it with a firearm, much less a sword.

As soon as she was alone in the small quarters for a person of her rank, she went into the bathroom and looked in the mirror. The dye in her silver hair was gone, exposing her identity to the Captain and crew of the Frigate. She sat her crystal on the small desk in the room and activated it. This time her mother answered.

"Mother look at me. I've been discovered because the dye in my hair washed out while hiding, waiting for rescue. Why didn't Grandmother tell me about my hair?"

Her grandmother leaned in over her mother.

"Because the image we were receiving was dark. We could barely recognize your face. There must have been something in the area distorting the image."

"Are you on Hollis Grandmother?"

"Yes, I came here as soon as your mother notified us."

"Mother, what am I to do now?"

"Jilena, the choice is yours, but the universe will soon know and in knowing who you are, they will know where your Father has been all these years. It will get crazy around here for a time, and once your siblings are recognized in their relationship to you, their lives will change, but all of you have been trained for this day. Take it one step at a time, one day at a time."

"Yes Mother. One day at a time."

Jilena broke the connection then looked at the kitten as it played with a ball someone had placed in the gage. She punched in the mess facility on the intercom and asked for a small bowl of milk for the kitten. What she received would feed four kittens, so she broke out her small bowl from her pack, poured some milk into it, then placed it in the container for the kitten. It sniffed it twice then began to lap it up with its coarse tongue.

A female Yeoman rapped on her door a few minutes later with a new uniform and advised Jilena she was to assist her during her stay aboard the Frigate. Jilena just sighed and told the Yeoman to make herself comfortable while she took a shower. Then she remembered she needed underwear and told the Yeoman what size to get her while she showered.

The Frigate's Maintenance Chief heard about the fangs and asked her for them. He told her he was going to clean them then string them for a necklace. She laughed and asked if he could deal with the pelt also. He said he could after he did some reading.

Jilena ate with the Captain and his senior officers in his stateroom for the evening meal where Captain advised her that he had been ordered to take her to Hayuta. She never hesitated when she told him that if she went directly to Hayuta, she would take his head and place it on a pike outside the Council Chambers. He would take her to Hollis and advise the Hayutan Council to leave her alone since by Federation Fleet regulations, she has thirty days survivor leave coming. After that she would consider entertaining the Council's request.

By the time they reached Hollis, the Chief had tanned and softened the pelt. Jilena named the kitten Ismael after her Great Uncle and decided to keep the animal if it could be trained to a litter box as a normal house cat. Only time would tell.

Department of Archaeology

Bellus University

For centuries, the scientists and scholars of Bellus had been attempting to decipher a gold tablet engraved with an ancient language unknown to the Bellusarians. The scholars held hope that once Bellus joined the Federation they would have help in deciphering the tablet, but it wasn't until Hayuta came into the picture since the Hayutan people were the original humans of the universe, not Earth which the Hayutans had seeded as an experiment.

For three decades, Professor Juozas Popkyn, a Hayutan scholar had been working on the tablet with Bellusarian scholars, trying to understand the bits and pieces of the tablet that had already been deciphered. It wasn't until he stumbled upon an obscure document of a centuries dead scholar that he found the key.

He hand wrote out the inscription on the tablet. Looked at it then went back to check what he had written to ensure that he had not made a mistake. What he read shook him enough that he hid the notes he had made, then asked his co-professor to work the tablet using the key he had found. First the key was checked then rechecked before his associate deciphered the tablet.

Both men agreed on the final results. After days of conversation, they determined that it was best they report that the tablet was undecipherable. They sealed the results of their research and locked them away until needed.

The tablet was a prophecy written over a thousand years before of what could come about for the universe, and Popkyn notated that half of the prophecy had already came true.

Reality

By the time Jilena completed her thirty days survivor's leave she came to the reality that Ismael would never be tame enough to allow contact with humans. It was suggested that having him neutered would reduce some of his aggressiveness, but she could not even consider that. She turned him over to an animal rescue service who would keep him until weened and eating meats then they would arrange for him to be placed back into the wilderness. Jilena told them not to place him on Hollis when they picked him up.

Several things happened while she was on leave. Using a convoluted method of figuring how to report and classify the injury she sustained from Ismael's mother. It was determined Jilena would not have been endangered by the Liger if the Raiders had not attacked the survey camp, then killed her protective detail. Therefore, her wounds were directly related to enemy action, so she was awarded a Wound Stripe for her uniform.

Jilena learned through her grandmother that there were seventeen other survivors of the attack on the survey camp. The one thing she did protest and lost was that the Fleet named the planet Jilena after her. She tried to convince them to name it after one of the Marines killed on the planet, but her argument fell upon deaf ears since her real identity had been discovered.

Her father took the Liger fangs and sliced them length ways and embedded them into the grips of her swords. With Ismael gone, she laid the Liger hide across her bed. It actually surprised her that the pelt was as large as it was. She rubbed her leg at the scars and though about how lucky she was to be alive.

When her leave was up, Jilena went to confront the Hayutan Council. But she did not go alone and that in itself made the Council nervous. When the ramp on her shuttle dropped,

Jilena walked down it in her Fleet Uniform with her Father and Grandmother following behind her, side by side also in uniform.

This was how they walked to the Council Chambers, through the hallways of the Palace. People in the halls just moved out of their way, flattening themselves against the walls as all three of the Royals were wearing their swords in defiance of Hayutan law concerning weapons in the Palace.

Before they arrived at the Council Chambers, they were intercepted by an elderly gentleman in tattered clothing and a mass of unkept graying hair. He bowed from his waist then stood in front of Jilena.

"Your Royal Highness, I beg your forgiveness for being impertinent and imposing upon you. I doubt that you remember me."

Jilena smiled at the old man.

"Professor Popkyn who taught my ancient language course at the university. What brings you back to Hayuta and to block my path?"

"Your Highness, I came to beg you not to renounce the throne."

"Professor, who has sent you to do this?"

"Princess Jilena, no one except my own conscious. I cannot tell you what I know, but it is vital that you do not renounce the throne."

"Come closer Professor and say what you fear."

He stepped closer.

"Your Highness, please I beg of you, I cannot explain why you must not renounce the throne, but in time, in your Royal Ancestors time, it will all become very clear to you."

"Professor Popkyn, what have you discovered?"

He bowed deeply at the waist.

"You may take my head Your Highness, but I cannot divulge what I have discovered."

Jilena looked at Popkyn, bent over, exposing his neck to her. She stepped forward, took him by the shoulders and raised him up.

"Professor Popkyn, do not concern yourself with losing your head. I shall take your advice to heart as I know you are a modest man of means and have not asked for anything to profit from this exchange. Go now as I must talk to the Council before I make my final decision."

Popkyn reached down, took her hand and kissed it.

"Thank you, Your Highness. May the Saints watch over you."

Popkyn shuffled off down the hallway as Jilena just watched him depart.

"Jilena, what did courses did he teach at the university?"

"Father, besides Ancient Languages, he taught Archaeology. If my memory serves me correctly he was working on the Golden Tablet also."

"I heard about that tablet while in Intelligence. The Fleet's code breakers took a shot at it without luck. Do you think he might have broken the code?"

"He's brilliant Father, but what could that tablet have to do with my renouncing the throne?"

"Jilena, if he was teaching on Bellus, he came a long way to risk his head to talk to you."

"Yes, Grandmother, that thought has crossed my mind too. Now let's go talk to the Council."

They had not been challenged until they reached the Council Chamber doors, when the Captain of the Guard stood in their way.

"Your Highness, it is forbidden to enter the Council Chambers with a weapon of any manner. You must surrender your blades, please."

Jilena smiled at him as she spoke in a quiet, yet firm manner.

"Captain, the only reason your head is still attached to your shoulders is because you ended that comment with please. Now stand aside before I remove your manhood."

The Captain's face paled as he considered his situation. The three Royals standing in front of him all who had used their blades in defense of their persons, and the fact that Princess Jilena had faced a Liger with only a blade was well known. He stepped aside and motioned to the Guards to open the doors for the Royals to pass through.

They were announced as they entered the chambers causing the Council to stand. Jilena walked to the head of the Council table and just stood with her Father to her left and Grandmother to her right. She never gave anyone on the Council a chance to speak.

"Ladies and Gentlemen, is this meeting being broadcast to the Hayutan people?"

"No, your Highness." The President responded.

"Activate the system, the Hayutan people need to hear my words."

Less than a minute later, an aide motioned from the back of the Chambers they were broadcasting.

"President Claiborne, Council, please be seated as what I have to say will not take much of your time."

She waited until everyone was seated.

"As I understand it, a declaration has been issued to accept my presence on the Hayutan Throne. I have given this much thought and spent hours in discussion with my Grandmother, Princess Lujayn and my Father, Prince Alexander. Princess Lujayn renounced the throne once she had the Principles of Leadership in place and formal elections held to give the Hayutan people proper representation. My Father renounced the throne, so he could live his life as he chose, and to prevent the Hayutan people from risking the loss of their power to elect and determine their future."

She paused to let her comments sink into the minds of the people.

"When I entered the Palace today, my thoughts were in following my ancestors path and decline the throne in favor of self-rule by the people. When Princess Lujayn sat on the throne in her final years of rule, it was mostly a ceremonial position. My Father foresaw the people desiring once again to be ruled by the Throne and renounced the Throne to prevent himself from being trapped upon it. Today I foresee the same situation, and even more so."

Jilena once more paused.

"At no time since I was discovered and reported to the Council have I communicated with the Council, nor has any attempt been made to communicate with me, which I am grateful for. But everything I have read or heard has told me the Council expects me to ascend the throne and rule of the Hayutan Worlds."

"As I said, I entered the Palace to renounce the throne, but a single individual, a person with no political agenda has begged me to ascend to the throne. This is an individual who first knew me only as Jilena Donovan, student. He offered his head to me for being impertinent in addressing me as I walked to these Chambers today. In doing so, he showed what it truly means to have self-rule. I cannot in good faith deny his request."

"Mister President, Ladies and Gentlemen of the Hayutan Council. I accept the Throne not for myself, but for the Hayutan People. I accept the Throne with exceptions which I do not and will not allow debate on."

Jilena watched the faces of the Council as she paused again in her speech.

"As Jilena Donovan, I took an oath to serve the Federation Fleet. Oaths should never be given lightly nor lightly broken. I still have over three years left on my contract with the Fleet and will not break my oath to serve the Federation in that capacity."

"As Princess Jilena Kaylani Borland, I must honor that oath because it is still the honorable thing to do. As the Throne of Hayuta, I expect the Council and Parliament of Hayuta to protect and encourage the Hayutan people in the principles of self-rule as set down in the Principles of Leadership, especially as I continue to fulfill my oath and service to the Fleet."

"I caution everyone who hears my voice today, do not require me to return to these Chambers to set right that which the people feel is in violation of the Principles of Leadership. I will appoint a secretary whose function will be to advise me of events and actions of the Council and Parliament while I am serving in the Fleet. That person will have access to any and all information and will attend all Council meetings in my absence. Hide nothing from this person and I will not have to take leave to return and correct the situation."

"I Princess Jilena Kaylani Borland do accept my position on the Throne of Hayuta. You have heard my voice, listened to my words. My word is my bond."

The President stood.

"Your Royal Highness, I speak for the Council in that we accept your bond, and conditions to it."

He began to clap and was joined by the rest of the Council as they rose from their seats. Jilena bowed to the Council and that was returned to her by the Council as they continued their applause. She turned and left the Chambers with her Father and Grandmother following. Jilena stopped at the doors and spoke to the Captain of the Guard.

"Captain, do you know the one known as Professor Popkyn?"

"Yes, your Highness, I am aware of this individual."

"Find him. He was in the Palace less than thirty minutes ago. He will be brought to me unharmed and as a gentleman. Do this now Captain. We shall be in the Royal apartments waiting for you to bring him to me."

"Yes, Your Highness." He left in a hurry talking into his communicator.

"Granddaughter, what are you thinking?"

"Not here Grandmother, wait until we are in your old apartment."

As soon as they entered the Royal apartments, Jilena took a small device from her belt pouch and walked around the sitting room, checking for bugging devices. She left it turned on and set it on the ornate coffee table as she took one of the chairs to sit in, while the others took the couch after unhooking their long swords for comfort.

"Grandmother, unlike you who had Kazimeras to deal with things between you and the old Council of Lords, I have no one. Now I doubt that Popkyn will ever divulge what drove him to confront me, to beg me to take the throne, especially since I remember him lecturing on the pitfalls of Royal rule verses Republican rule at the university. He was pro-Republican."

"Yes, Jilena, that would make a person think if they had more information, such as what caused him to change his position?"

"Exactly Grandmother. Now we know there is a small minority that does not want me on the throne, not because of me personally, but because of the Royal aspect of it all. You and Father have both witnessed what happens when a person of weak character gains authority while in service. It can destroy a good command in a short period of time. I suspect if we study history deep enough, we shall find the same with Royals and those they rule. The opposite can be said of Count Conrad Denoyelles' father. He ruled with an iron fist."

"Yes Daughter, and he played one Royal off on another, using them to increase his own power base, while hindering the growth of his subjects."

"Yes Father, I'm aware of that. Anyway, to answer Grandmother's earlier question, I am going to appoint Professor Popkyn as my secretary much as Count Conrad appointed Lord Strahovski as his Chancellor. A person outside the political arena."

Princess Lujayn and her Father laughed at the concept Jilena had just weakly described. They talked more until there was a knock on the apartment doors, then it opened with the Captain of the Guard announcing Professor Popkyn. Popkyn was escorted to the sitting Royals by the Captain, who bowed, then left after Jilena motioned for him to leave. Popkyn was shaking as he stood before the Royals.

"Professor Popkyn, did you hear my speech in the Council Chambers?"

"Yes, your Highness, it was broadcast across the quad as I was leaving the palace grounds, My Lady."

"Did you notice I mentioned you, not by name, but as the person who stood and begged me to take the throne?"

"Yes, your Highness, I did."

"What do you think I am going to do now Professor?"

"Princess Jilena, you will do what you desire, but nothing you can do to me will cause me to reveal why I came to you, said what I said to you. I'm sorry My Lady, but I cannot explain my plea any further than I already have."

"Professor Popkyn, I want your head this day, but I want it firmly affixed to your shoulders. As you heard, I need a secretary to act for me with the Council while I am off with the Fleet. I desire you to be that secretary."

"Your Highness, but I am only a minor scholar, not worthy of such a position."

"I shall decide if you are worthy Professor. Will you accept the bond I place upon you?"

"Yes, My Princess, I am humbled and will accept the bond."

Jilena stood and walked to Popkyn, then drew her dagger from her belt and offered it to him hilt first.

"A blood oath Professor. I remember you lecturing in the university on them and the power they have to tie two people together."

He looked at the blade in her hand, took it and made a cut to his left hand, deep enough to draw blood, but not deep enough to disable his hand.

"You have my oath My Lady."

"Thank you, Professor. Now one other thing. Father would you call the Guard in, all of them."

Alexander never spoke as he left the couch, went to the door and instructed all of the guard in the hall to enter. He saw two people walking and instructed them into the apartment since he felt he knew what Jilena had on her mind. Once everyone was where they could see Jilena and Popkyn, she instructed Popkyn to kneel before her. She stepped back and drew her long sword which made several people look as if they were about to witness an execution. Instead, she laid her blade on his left shoulder.

"Professor Popkyn, you have served the students of Hayuta and Bellus for decades as an honorable and honest teacher of ancient knowledge."

She placed the blade on his right shoulder.

"You have accepted a bond between yourself and myself which only death can break."

She placed the blade on top of his balding head.

"Arise Lord Popkyn, arise Lord Secretary to the Throne of Hayuta, and let the witnesses here today know that I have complete trust and faith in the bond we now hold. Arise Lord Popkyn and assume your duties to the Throne of Hayuta."

Popkyn weakly stood up and bowed to Jilena. Her Grandmother spoke before anyone else could break the sudden silence in the room.

"Captain of the Guard. There are apartments connected to this one for handmaids and cook. Lord Popkyn is to have one

40

along with a helper of his choice and a cook so he is not to be bothered by the Palace kitchen. See to his moving into the apartment of his choice and at no time is the Lord Secretary to leave the confines of the apartment without escort. Make the arrangements today, before the sun sets on the Palace."

"Yes, Princess Lujayn."

Jilena gave Popkyn a final instruction.

"Go Lord Popkyn with the Captain of the Guard and collect your belongings. We have much to do and little time to attend to it as I must return to the Fleet to fulfill my oath of service."

Facilities Engineer

When Fleet Officers receive orders transferring them post to another, unless the ship they are serving on is heading towards their new posting, they hop-scotch across the universe until they arrive at their new posting. In the case of Lieutenant Commander Jilena Donovan, as she insisted on keeping her original name, she arrived in the newest Hayutan Heavy Cruiser which she christened the Wyatt, after the Marine team leader that was killed trying to protect her during the attack on the survey camp.

The Hayutan Government had stood firm in that she have a means of traveling to and from Hayuta as part of her Royal duties. The ship came with one hundred, handpicked Hayutan Marines who had sworn a blood oath to protect the Throne, meaning Jilena's person, as had the crew of the Wyatt.

The Wyatt and Marines created a problem for the Fleet Command as they had no facilities for the personal or place in orbit or on the ground to park the Cruiser while Jilena was on the surface. Her orders put her in the Fleet's Facilities Engineering office in the number eight slot with one of her functions to act as the Headquarters Facilities Engineer.

Her assignment put her in charge of the maintenance and upkeep of the Fleet Headquarters and all of its attachments to include the Fleet Academy Facilities. Any request for repairs or improvements went across her desk.

The Denoyelles family came to the rescue for the crew of the Wyatt by building a heavy-duty landing pad next to the dividing fence between the Fleet area and the Denoyelles shipyards. The quarters for the crew and Marines aboard the Wyatt were more than sufficient for living on the ground, so no barracks were needed, but several buildings were put up for entertainment purposes.

Jilena went to work daily with at least one Hayutan Marine in escort and she had to make them stay at the Engineering buildings entrance portal, so he would not be standing outside her office door all day.

Six months after she assumed her duties, she was asked to survey all existing port facilities to ensure that the reports and account expenditures were being properly reported. The Fleet had her scheduled to hop from one planet to another on freighters and warships passing from one planet to another. She was calm when she advised them she would be taking the Wyatt since it would be following her wherever she went, so why wait for a freighter since she had her own ship, and better living quarters on that ship. The Fleet sent out a notice of her tour and that she would be arriving on a Hayutan ship.

It took Jilena nearly a year to make the tour using the Wyatt, where if she had used the Fleet's plan, it would have taken a minimum of another eight months. She filed her reports for each base from the Wyatt enroute to the next while sleeping alone. She had not taken a lover for a single night since she had returned to duty. Jilena was concerned about how her new position was attracting suitors that would want more than she was willing to give.

Jilena was going over an overview of the reports she had filed as the Wyatt was in transit to Bellus before going on to Denoyelles. There were minor discrepancies in the reports she had filed and within the overview, it appeared that all of the discrepancies could be traced back to one construction company. The Jaworski Company from New Earth.

The nature of the discrepancies varied from contract to contract and seemed minor until put together under one package. They totaled over six point four million credits, enough to construct a small outpost. Jilena wrote her final report and transmitted it to Fleet Headquarters expressing a need to audit the Jaworski Company for their over charges and bidding practices.

Two weeks later, the Wyatt was making its approach to Bellus to enter orbit when they were approached by a freighter also maneuvering into the pattern when at eight hundred kilometers, the freighter unleashed a dozen missiles at the Wyatt.

The Wyatt's newest automated defense systems recognized the threat and immediately raised its defensive shielding and activated the anti-missile defense systems. All twelve missiles were destroyed before they could come in contact with the shielding and the Captain ordered the freighter disabled and a boarding party to stand by to take the ship.

It only took minutes for the Wyatt's gunnery crew to knock out the engines of the freighter and as the two assault boats were disembarking to take their Marines over to board the freighter, the freighter self-destructed in a massive fireball.

Jilena was standing on the bridge, watching as this played out on the screen having gone to the bridge as soon as the missile warning alarm had sounded. She just stood there watching the expanding fireball of the freighter wondering why they had been attacked inside Bellus Space.

The Wyatt's Captain turned back to speak to his Yeoman when he saw that Jilena was on the Bridge.

"Excuse me Your Highness, what are you doing on the Bridge during Battle Stations?"

"I have no assigned post Captain Glanville for Battle Stations and felt this is where I should be instead of hiding in my stateroom."

"Sensors, do we have a solid track on those inbound missiles?"

"Aye, Captain, three had the bridge targeted."

"Thank you, Sensors. Now your Highness, if our automated systems had not performed to specification, you would be dead with the rest of us. Or seriously injured in the passageway between your stateroom and the bridge. If you desire to watch events unfold during Battle Stations, then the safest place is in Combat."

"Captain, does this ship belong to me?"

"Yes, your Highness it does."

"Then should I not be setting an example to my crew instead of hiding in my stateroom or Combat?"

"Your Highness, your logic is commendable but if we were going into battle, with advance knowledge of the fight in front of us, my place would be in Combat to fight the ship from there as per Federation and Hayutan Fleet regulations. And since you so stated before the Hayutan Council when you ascended the Throne that you are also a serving Fleet Officer, I will make this simple for you, My Lady."

He paused for a moment.

"Yeoman, insure my next statements are entered in to the ship's log and transmitted to the Hayutan Council immediately."

"Aye Captain."

"Lieutenant Commander Donovan, the curtesy of the bridge is extended to you only during those times we are not at Battle Stations. If you feel the need to present an appearance before the crew during that time, you will report to Combat Control and stand by there. I hereby direct the Marine Security Detachment responsible for your safety to physically take you to either your stateroom or to Combat in the case of you being elsewhere in the ship at the sounding of Battle Stations. When I say physically, I mean if need be, they will pick you up and throw you over their shoulders to take you to safety."

Captain Glanville had a grin on his face.

"Lieutenant Commander Donovan, do I need to explain my orders to you?"

"No Captain Glanville, you do not. I shall take my leave of the Bridge now."

"Yes, Please Lieutenant Commander, and do not let the hatch get in your way."

"Don't you mean don't let it hit me in the ass on the way out?"

"That too Commander." He said with a smile.

Procedure for entering into a low planetary orbit or landing on the surface required that all weapon systems be placed in a safe mode. This included the automated systems. Captain Glanville was not going to risk his ship or Princess Jilena in case of another attack while achieving a low orbit or landing so he selected a high orbit and announced to planetary control of same and that their weapons were not safed.

Jilena had barely walked into her stateroom when her crystal communicator linked to Lord Popkyn's began beeping. She sat at her desk and activated her crystal.

"Yes, Lord Popkyn?"

"Your Highness, are you well?"

"I am, thank you. Is there something bothering you?"

"Your Highness, when the Wyatt went to Battle Stations, the Council was informed of their status and I was summoned to the Council Chambers. The Council is concerned with your safety your Highness and asked that you return to Hayuta."

"I am safe Lord Popkyn. No, I shall not return to Hayuta as I still have my duties to perform with the Fleet. Also, I am at

Bellus at the request of the Council of Bellus. I shall attend to their request as quickly as I can then transit on to Denoyelles. Advise the Council of my actions and thank them for their concerns for my safety."

"Yes, My Lady. Now something else if it is safe to talk?"

"Go ahead."

"Princess, as you are aware, there is a faction here on Hayuta that does not like an occupant on the throne. This is of minor concern since they did vote to accept you and the conditions of your ascending to the throne. But our agents have picked up rumblings throughout the Federation of dissatisfaction with the Federation government."

"Lord Popkyn, there have always been dissent in the Federation."

"Yes, My Lady, but it seems to be strengthening. The articles your ancestor, Count Conrad laid down over two centuries ago   have been weakened with legislation. The Rebels your Sainted Grandmother fought is a clue to that."

He paused for only a moment.

"Your Highness please consider what happens over the next few days as a sign of what is to come. The current Duke Denoyelles is a very honorable man, but he is six generations separated from the Count, where you are only five generations. If you are so honored to be offered a place in history, accept it without pause. I wish I could say more, but I am oath bound to silence and I may have said more than I should have."

"Jouzas, is this part of what you could not tell me in the Palace before I accepted the throne?"

"Yes, my Princess. I have said too much already, but yes, it is."

"Jouzas…."

"My head is yours to take at your leisure My Lady, but it is a small sacrifice to make if I am right."

"We shall talk again Lord Popkyn. Until then, rest yourself, you look tired. And that is a Royal command."

"Yes, My Lady, I shall. Thank you."

Jilena broke the connection and leaned back in her chair. What has Popkyn discovered in his decades of research that scares a scholar to the point of offering his life to see that the results of his research is complete? That was the only thought in her mind as she tried to piece together what had been happening over the decades with the Federation. She needed to look deeper into the Federation to see what she could learn.

The Council of Bellus

To take Jilena to the surface of Bellus, the Wyatt launched four armored assault boats, each full to capacity with the exact number of male and female occupants. This was to confuse any sensors looking for the craft carrying her to the surface. On the way down, the lead boat was changed several times so no one could guess which carried the Princess.

The first boat landed and the Marines from it moved out and secured the immediate area as the boat lifted allowing the second boat to land. The Council of Bellus was standing on the Cathedral steps as they watched events unfolding before them, unsure what to do as both Bellusarian Marines and Rangers just stood back having been informed the Hayutans meant no harm but would not tolerate any harm to the Princess.

As the second boat was off loading its Marine cargo, two Marines from the first group detached themselves and walked to the steps of the Cathedral. The tallest of the two removed their helmet, exposing her fiery red hair and silver stripe through it.

"Council of Bellus, my apologizes for this show, but the Captain and crew of the Wyatt is concerned for my safety and I could not fight all of them. This was their idea, not mine."

A tall gentleman separated himself from the crowd and took one step down closer to her.

"Your Royal Highness, I am Edon Garrick, and I am Chancellor of Bellus. We welcome you back to our humble world even if you must return in such a manner."

Jilena looked the Chancellor over. He was tall, slender, with dark hair and she thought to herself that he wasn't so much handsome as he was pretty. She had not been with a man since before the survey camp and this man caused her to rethink her celibacy.

"Lord Garrick, I thank you for your welcome." She tapped the side of her helmet. "Pardon me, but I keep getting these messages from my Marines to get out of the open and under cover. Shall we get out of the open and into the Cathedral?"

Garrick laughed.

"Certainly, Your Highness. Right this way please."

He stepped aside and indicated the steps. The crowd split apart as Jilena and her Yeoman took the steps two at a time and entered the Cathedral's large double doors with Garrick and the Council following behind her.

Inside the Cathedral, Garrick once again spoke for the Council.

"You Highness, let us take you to the Royal apartments and find suitable clothing for you to sit and meet with the Council."

"Lord Garrick, I find these clothes suitable, but we also have our uniforms in our packs, so yes, give us a place to change then we can meet with the Council. Yeoman Sacheverell goes where I go. She keeps notes, so I do not misremember things of importance."

"I understand Your Highness. Please, follow me."

At the apartments, Garrick opened the door for them and ushered them in, following behind them while leaving the door open.

"You Highness, these are the apartments of your ancestor, Princess Kaya. No one has used these rooms since the passing of Princess Kaya, but they have been maintained as they were then for the expected occasion as this. If you need anything, there is an intercom on the desk properly marked for your convenience. I'll leave you now to change and refresh yourselves. Just press the Page button when you are ready to meet with the Council."

"Thank you, Lord Garrick. We should not be long."

Once alone, Yeoman Sacheverell spoke up.

"Goodness Commander, Lord Garrick is so handsome it almost hurts to look at him and his voice is like honey on a breakfast cake."

From the first day that Sacheverell reported as Jilena's Yeoman, Jilena required her to only address her as Commander since it was easier to use plus with minor exceptions, the work she was doing was in the capacity of her Fleet rank, not her Royal position.

"Sabella, I'm sure his wife thinks the same."

"He's not married or mated Commander."

"Then try not to injure him if you can get him on the sheets. Now we have things to do."

Jilena changed while thinking about what Sabella had said and felt the urge to find out what kind of man he really was. But she pushed that thought back as this was neither the time or place to end her drought. She brushed out her hair, just letting it fall to her shoulders thinking once out of the Fleet, she would just let it grow as long as she could tolerate.

They were escorted to the Council Chambers by four Bellusarian Royal Guards. Jilena entered the room to see everyone standing in front of their seats with two seats open for them. But the one at the end of the large conference table was throne like in appearance.

"Princess Jilena, you chair awaits you." Lord Garrick indicated the ornate chair.

Jilena looked around the room to see a plain chair like the others were to use off in the corner. She pulled the ornate chair back away from the table, then went to get the plain chair. An aide moved to help her but she waved him off as she drug the plain chair to the end of the table then sat down.

Garrick chuckled, as he watched her sit down.

"Your Highness, history tells us that your ancestor, Prince Michael hated that ornate chair as it represented the Throne of Bellus."

"Lord Garrick, in case you have missed it, I am in the uniform of a Federation Lieutenant Commander, not the Royal robes of a Princess. Shall we dispense with titles here today as I am simply Jilena Donovan, Lieutenant Commander in the Federation Fleet."

Garrick picked up a leather-bound folder and fingered it for a moment before speaking.

"Commander Donovan, we, the Council, are concerned about the attack on your ship yesterday. Our Orbital Control Center shows the IFF on that freighter to belong to the Atkinson Company here on Bellus. But in conferring with Atkinson, that freighter is on the Western Rim, picking up freight at this very moment. The Managing Director of Atkinson says he has talked to the Captain of the Freighter Selina and has confirmed its location."

"I find this very interesting that whomever orchestrated that attack would use the IFF of an Atkinson freighter."

"How so Commander?"

"Because my Father owns Atkinson along with the Dubois Shipping Company. I thought you knew that?"

"No Commander, it seems we do not. But yes, now it seems even more interesting."

"Lord Garrick, before you get too deep into my Father's holdings, I wish to advise you that it is all legal which you will find once you dig deep into the Atkinson and Dubois charters.

Now I will need a copy of your IFF data on that ship to present to the Federation Fleet, so they can investigate the attack upon a Hayutan ship inside Federation space."

"If you will allow, we shall send that information along with the statement of the Atkinson manager, so we can also speak of our dislike for what happened above Bellus."

"You have my permission and please copy the Wyatt in that transmission."

"We shall, thank you. Now the reason we asked you to come to Bellus. Commander, the Federation is at a crossroads. We Bellusarians view events at the Federation Capital as being in favor of some worlds over others. This is not what your ancestor, Count Conrad established when he reformed the Federation. We of Bellus are not being harmed by some of the tariffs and taxes levied over the past decade, but in time, we may find ourselves in that situation. Our Ambassador has voted time and time again against such regulations, but he has warned us only time will tell before we find ourselves a target."

"Edon, may I call you Edon?"

"Certainly Commander."

"Thank you. Edon, Bellus has close ties to the Denoyelles family, has your Ambassador spoken with the current Duke?"

"Commander, yes they have spoken. The Duke has also stood against those regulations and has expressed that he feels the only reason the Denoyelles family has not been subjected to them is because of the shipyards and factories the Federation needs to maintain the Fleet and other projects."

"I don't know what I can do without more information and studying the problem. Edon, you keep fingering that folder as if it is hot, would you care to move this conversation along?"

Garrick laughed.

"Spoken like a true Engineer. No time for nonsense. Alright Commander, let's move this along."

He opened the folder and looked around the table. Jilena noticed everyone was looking at her, not him.

"Lord Prince Mikhail still living and overseeing the rule of Keres, has refused to take any steps to claim the Throne of Bellus. Princess Lujayn and Prince Alexander have renounced the Thrones of Bellus and Hayuta. Your Highness Princess Jilena Borland, it is the will of the Council of Bellus with the support of the people of Bellus that you accept the Throne of Bellus, uniting Bellus with Hayuta."

"Why should I undertake such a thing Lord Chancellor?"

"Because within a decade, we feel the Federation will collapse. With our two world systems united, we will be able to survive the collapse."

"Would a treaty between our two systems be enough to unite the worlds without my taking the Throne?"

"We have considered this, and it is possible, but with you on the Throne, it will strengthen that merging of worlds. And the fact that you are in a sense a Denoyelles, that will make the joining even stronger."

Jilena was now wondering what Popkyn knew that he was not telling her. Did he know the Council of Bellus was going to offer her the Throne? As she was considering Garrick's words, a Royal Guard entered and handed Garrick a message. Garrick read the message then looked at Jilena.

"Commander, we have a Lancer warship entering our system with a Centaurian named Ismael aboard requesting an audience with you here in the Cathedral."

Jilena smiled as she responded.

54

"Please tell Uncle Ismael he can land with just his boat crew and visit me in the Royal apartments. Council of Bellus, please allow me some time to consider your request. This is a lot to consider and I am just a Fleet Engineer. Excuse me now, I need to think this through before I can give you my answer."

The Council stood, with Garrick coming to her end of the table. He leaned close and whispered to her.

"Uncle Ismael?"

"Yes, he is the only man who would only use his name to contact me, instead of his name and rank. Advise the Guard to see him directly to the apartments as soon as he is on the ground."

"Yes Commander, it will be done."

In the apartment, Jilena went directly to the wine service, smelled one bottle then poured a large glass before stretching out on one of the couches.

"Commander, do you think it is wise to drink from their selection without having it tested first?"

"Sabella, at this point, if it is poisoned, it is doing me a favor. It's as if the Universe has suddenly turned against me. The only crime I have committed is being born with a drop of Royal blood and this damned silver hair. I once thought this silver hair was great, but now I understand my Father even more on why he rubbed ash in his hair each morning, so it would only look like unnatural gray hair."

"But Commander, it is a great honor the Bellusarians are offering you. To unite two people under one banner."

"Yes Sabella, I am aware of the honor, and also aware of the responsibility. Please, give me some time to think."

"Yes Commander."

Three hours later there was a knock on the door and Sabella went to the doors, then looked back to see Jilena standing, waiting for her to open them. On the other side was a Centaurian, dressed in a Lancer uniform. Jilena looked at the nearly gray fur of her Great-Uncle Ismael and thought he must have been fierce looking in his youth. Ismael walked into the apartment with a slight limp. Jilena moved to him and greeted him with a warm embrace.

"Ismael, it warms my heart to see you."

"Mine also my child, but sadly this is not a social visit. Jilena we need to talk."

"Certainly Uncle, please sit, get off that leg."

"Thank you."

They both sat down on the couch as Jilena held one of Ismael's hands.

"What brings you to Bellus to meet with me?"

"I bring a message from the Duke. Ascend onto the Throne of Bellus. Events are taking shape in the shadows that concerns him, and even with the power of the Denoyelles family, he is afraid he cannot stop what is just over the horizon."

"Did he explain what is over the horizon?"

"No, my child, but there are rumors of war. Civil war. Factions within the Federation may soon rebel against what many consider the unjust laws and regulations being forced upon them. He said it is not unlike the times of the Count, but this time, it will not be as peaceful in collapsing."

"What can I do? I'm only an Engineer, not a command trained officer."

"Jilena, by taking the Bellus Throne, you will become the next in line for the Dukedom. Duke Thomas has no children as you know, and he has no faith in the ones who will jockey for his chair if anything happens to him."

"What of the Centaurian people?"

"It is known that your mother is Centaurian by birth, and that your Father was born with the Centaurian fur covering his body. The cloak of fur no longer matters as it is a personal choice, but it is the birth and schooling that matters. Your mother and step-mothers schooled you in the ways of a Centaurian. That schooling is evidence by the Liger fangs you wear on the handles of your swords. And your compassion is shown by the fact you did not kill the kitten when others would have."

"So, you are just a messenger this day my Uncle?"

"No, I have with me one hundred hand-picked Centaurian Lancers who are prepared to swear a blood oath in your presences to protect your life with theirs. Jilena, what is unknown to the Federation is that the Lancers have been in service to the Denoyelles family since moving to Hanover under Count Conrad. This is another concern of Duke Thomas in once he passes and another takes the chair, that fact will be known to the Federation. A fact best not divulged in passing."

"So, if I take the Throne, and Duke Thomas is assassinated, I suddenly become the most powerful person in the Universe. Holy Saints, this is too much my dear Uncle."

"Jilena, the House of Hanover, the Thrones of Hayuta and Bellus, and the people of Hawkings will certainly make you the one person that any threat to the Federation will have to deal with. You will have a targeting dot on your forehead."

Jilena just looked at Ismael, unable to answer."

"But Jilena, the Thrones will still be united, and if anything, the worlds will remain neutral until the last ember of rebellion grows cold. From those ashes a new Federation can be born. That is something to consider."

"I don't know Ismael. I just don't know."

"Jilena, think about this then. What happened yesterday was an attempt to kill you, plain and simple as that. I don't know who you've upset or scared, but killing you is the only thing that makes sense in that attack yesterday. Accept the Bellus Throne and you will wrap yourself in layers of protection."

"I'm just an Engineer. Who could I have upset to the point they wanted me dead?"

"Could you have seen something, anything during your inspection tour that might have scared someone?"

Jilena thought for a moment then smiled.

"Yes, but still not enough to want me dead, yet, what if I found was hiding something else? Something they only thought I might have seen?"

"Well they failed yesterday, but that does not mean they will not try again tomorrow."

"Uncle Ismael, go back to the ship, tell the Lancers I do not need a blood oath, their word is their bond. What of the ship and crew?"

"Jilena, it is one of the new Churchill class attack carriers. It has ten armored assault boats and is gunned up like a heavy destroyer. The crew is mixed and will follow you anywhere. They also have agreed to take the blood oath."

"Then pass on to the crew I accept their word as I do the Lancers. Go, take care of this now. I have other things to think on and do before I take another step. Prepare a section to drop upon my command to assume my security, but not until I give the word."

Ismael leaned over and kissed her on both cheeks before standing.

"As you wish my Princess."

"Ismael, what of you? What are your plans now?"

"I'm going home to play with my grandchildren and plant a garden. Jilena, I've been doing this long before your grandmother lost her virginity. It's time for me to retire and enjoy my brood."

"Then go with my love and blessings. Thank you, Uncle Ismael."

He smiled and gave her a slight bow, then left her thinking he would have been perfect to serve her here while she was gone, but he had earned his time to enjoy the rest of his life.

She considered using one of her siblings as her Secretary here on Bellus, but that would put them directly in harm's way. Then she had another thought which scared her. She went to the desk and activated her crystal.

"Yes, Your Highness?"

"Popkyn, inform the Council I want a minimum of a platoon of Marines to protect my grandparent's and another my parents. And I want them in the air today."

"Yes, yes, Your Highness, I shall do that right now."

She deactivated her crystal and went back to the couch and stretched out, letting herself relax as she thought about how her life was changing.

"Sabella."

"Yes Commander?"

"Contact, no, go see Lord Garrick. See if he is free for dinner. Express to him it will be an informal business dinner.

Then go to the kitchen and develop a menu please. Nothing heavy, but flavorful would be nice. And another bottle of that wine if you please."

"Right away Commander. Are you going to be alright here alone?"

"Unless there is a hidden passageway to allow an assassin in, yes, tell the guards to admit no one but yourself. Tell them I have a headache and resting."

"Certainly Commander. I'll be back as quick as I can."

"Thank you, Sabella."

When Sabella returned, Jilena was still on the couch but not asleep. She was still deep in thought about where her life was at and the crossroad she had to decide on which path to take. Ismael was right, she was now a target because of something she has seen or thought to have seen. But she could not fathom what that could have been to send men on what was basically a suicide mission to not only kill her, but the crew of her ship.

Was there something about her being on the Throne of Hayuta? Does someone out there that did not want her to take the throne of Bellus? She would have to discuss this with Edon over dinner. Her thoughts were interrupted by Sabella.

"Commander, our luggage is in your bed chambers. I've moved mine to the handmaiden's apartment. Unless you need me, I would like to change and take in the local atmosphere."

"Who is he Sabella?"

"A Sergeant in the Royal Guard."

"Well that was quick. I suspect he is handsome and well built."

"Commander, he is neither, but at least he had the courage to ask me to dinner."

"Can you get to your apartment without going through the main bed chamber?"

"Yes Commander."

"Good, I'd hate to injure you if you came in late from an eventful evening by waking me up from a sound sleep."

"If you say so Commander."

"Sabella, right now I need answers and Lord Garrick seems to be the one to give them to me due to his position here on Bellus. As far as his position on my body, that is not on the menu tonight."

"Yes Commander."

"And Sabella, do not go unarmed."

"Yes Commander."

Jilena looked at her clothing and decided since tonight was a business meeting to wear slacks and a blouse instead of one of the dresses which showed a lot of cleavage. She had the kitchen's steward set a small table, so the conversation would be more personal and dismissed the three waiters who were assigned to keep their glasses full and plates full. Jilena did not want any witnesses to what might be spoken between her and Garrick.

She swept the room with a bug detector and then sat it on the table, so she could view it as they talked over dinner. Jilena was concerned that others might listen in on their conversation and since she still had doubts about ascending the throne, she did not want anyone later doubting her reasons for accepting it.

Garrick arrived on schedule with Jilena waiting by the table for him. Their greetings were informal, and he waited until she was seated before taking his own chair at the table. The table was small enough they could pass serving dishes back and forth to each other without having to stand, and she watched her indicator to see if he was carrying any listening devices.

She learned he had been an electrical engineer before being drafted into public life and he still worked at the trade when government duties allowed. Jilena asked him questions concerning trade and economy, questions she could have had Sabella research, but she wanted to hear the answers from Garrick, which she would check in the morning since many times, what is reported is not reality.

Jilena switched to the problems with the Federation Congress about half way through the meal and found Garrick had some bitter comments concerning trade with some planets because of the tariffs placed on those worlds by the Congress. In that conversation she knew that she was missing something, but did not further question Garrick on the subject as she thought she had the information at her fingertips.

It was during the dessert phase of dinner that she changed directions in the conversation from business to a more personal nature.

"Edon, a man of your looks, and charm, why is it you are not married?"

"I was Jilena, I lost her about eight years ago in a horrific accident that also took the lives of six others."

"Oh! I am so sorry to hear that Edon, forgive me for bringing it up."

"It's alright Jilena. I mourned my loss for about three years then woke up to the fact I still had a life to live."

"And you have yet to find anyone to replace her?"

"Yes and no."

The look he gave her was one she was not expecting, but one that changed her mind about what to do after dessert. She reached her hand across the table and he took it. As he held her hand she knew how this night would end unless he decided otherwise.

"Edon, I have not been with a man for nearly three years. The night is still young."

"Jilena, let me be completely honest with you. I find you very desirable and the thought of spending the night with you is a very pleasant one. But this night is all we can have. It does not matter if you take the throne or not to me at this junction, on a personal basis that is, but I refuse to fall in love with you only to lose you to an assassin. I've seen the intelligence and even if we do not know who is behind the attempt on your life, you are marked for death unless you, and the people who are protecting you are very careful. I've lost one love, I will not lose another."

"Thank you for your honesty Edon. I have to admit that my plans for tonight did not include you in my bed, but after talking to you, visiting with you, my desires have changed my mind. If you do not wish to stay with me tonight, I understand."

"But Jilena, that is the problem. I do want to stay."

"Then I think we are done here, shall we move on to a more enjoyable venue?"

Jilena stood in the massive bathroom drying herself from the long, hot shower she took looking at the marks on her body from the previous night thinking she had entertained better, but Edon had worked hard at satisfying her needs. Yes, it was a satisfying evening even if she had not enjoyed Edon in bed. Her mind was made up about the throne. Her thoughts were interrupted by Sabella speaking to her from the doorway.

"Well Commander, it looks like you had an enjoyable evening?"

Jilena looked over at Sabella.

"Yeah, well I guess the menu got changed and I became dessert. How was your evening out?"

"It ended the same as yours Commander. For a small man, he was not small. I may not walk normal for a couple days."

Jilena laughed.

"Good for you Sabella. Now today, we dress Fleet formal."

"Very good Commander. May I ask you a question?"

"Certainly."

"Were you having me watched last night?"

"Explain that"

"It seemed no matter where we went last night, there were Centaurians near."

Jilena looked at Sabella.

"No Sabella, but I suspect my Uncle Ismael had his hand in that. You are privy to my secrets and now that I think about it, kidnapping you for those secrets would put me in a bad situation. I refuse to restrict your off-duty movements Sabella, but I think caution is called for."

"Yes Commander, and I appreciate your consideration. But after last night, I'm good for some time. Especially if I can learn to walk normally again."

Once more Jilena laughed.

"Yes, I have had a few of those days myself. Now, let's see what the kitchen has prepared for breaking our fast."

At ten that morning, Bellus time, Jilena walked into the Council Chambers and just stood at the end of the table. She

64

smiled to herself that the plain chair was still in place from the previous day.

"Council of Bellus, is this meeting being broadcast?"

"Yes, Commander Donovan." Edon answered for the Council.

"Ladies and Gentlemen of the Council. Citizens of Bellus. I have given your request to ascend the Throne of Bellus much thought, and I have spoken to others whose advice I respect. I make my next statement with the people's wishes and advice of my advisors."

She paused.

"I, Jilena Kaylani Borland, Princess of Hayuta, heir to the Protectorate of Keres, do accept your wishes and desires and accept the Throne of Bellus. As with Hayuta, I shall appoint a Secretary to sit in my place when absent to keep me advised of the Councils decisions as I entrust them to continue the fine work they have been doing for Bellus. I hope that I do not betray the trust the people of Bellus has placed before me. I am Princess Jilena Kaylani Borland, and my word is my bond."

Ripples

Immediately upon her accepting the Throne of Bellus, Lancers began landing in the square in front of the Cathedral. They made no effort in replacing the Royal Guard, but for every Guard on duty was a fully, suited up Centaurian Lancer by his side. The word quickly spread that Jilena was being protected by the fiercest warriors in the Federation.

When Jilena was asked about the color or colors of her Royal Guards livery, it dawned on her that she had not given it any thought and her Hayutan Guards wore standard uniforms. She communicated with her Grandmother before deciding on her livery. It would be Scarlett and Gold with Pewter trim. The Pewter was the color of the Denoyelles family and would accent the Scarlett coats of the guards.

Once the Council had sealed her ascension to the throne, she changed into more suitable clothing and move into the Throne Room to accept Ambassador's from various worlds who wished to meet and greet her. After several proposed alliances with Bellus outside of the Federation's restrictions, Jilena moved from the Throne and had a table set in front of the Throne platform with two standard chairs for her and her guest. If they just wished to greet her, she stood by the table and was cordial in her statements to them. But if they wished to talk about alliances or trade agreements, she allowed them fifteen minutes and they sat at the table, which she expressed was an inform discussion since all agreements still had to go through the Council of Bellus. Jilena noted that most were victims of the Federation's oppressive tariffs and trade laws.

As she was talking to the Ambassador from Winslow, a frontier world, she noticed a Lancer officer enter and walk to within about ten paces from the table, then assumed a position they called Parade Rest. Jilena only took notice of the Lancers rank so she did not lose focus on what the Ambassador was saying. As with the others, she told the Ambassador to work up a proposal and get it into the hands of Lord Garrick.

As the Ambassador was walking away, she motioned to the Lancer to come forward as it appeared he was needing to see her. This time she got a better look at him. He was tall and even from a distance she could see his bright blue eyes beneath his black eyebrows. His beard was shaped like her Father's, only coming down the jaw line to the edge of his mouth, then a beard and mustache. His neck was clean of fur but what she saw was thick and black. His build looked as if he could lift an assault boat without help.

"May I have a moment of your time, Your Highness?" His voice was deep and rich in tone.

"Certainly Captain. Who are you and your position?"

"Gannaway, My Lady, Tamika Gannaway. I am the Captain of your Lancer Guard, and yes, Your Highness, I am related to the Sergeant Major. But you can rejoice in that you are not related to me, My Lady."

Jilena laughed.

"Yes, Uncle Ismael is a legend in his own time. What can I do for you Captain Gannaway?"

"May I approach so I do not have to speak too loud?"

"Yes, you may."

He stepped closer.

"My Lady, within the hour of your announcement of ascending the throne of Bellus, two men disguised as Fleet Facilities Maintenance attempted to gain access to your living quarters on Denoyelles. They were stopped, questioned and taken into custody when an explosive device was discovered during a search of their persons and tool boxes."

"Who took them into custody Captain?"

"Lancers, Ma'am. Your quarters have been under surveillance since the attempt on your life while on the Wyatt, My Lady."

"Where are these men now?"

"Last report was on an assault boat heading for Hanover and Lancer Headquarters, so the Psych Docs can shift through their brains to find out who sent them."

Jilena thought for a moment before responding.

"Captain, advise Lancer HQ to keep you advised of the smallest detail and you Sir, will advise me as quickly as possible, even in my apartment, regardless of hour."

"Yes, My Lady, but I would hate to interrupt some important meeting such as you had last night."

"Captain, last night was a one-time meeting. Damn, you have been hanging around Ismael, haven't you?"

She laughed then Tamika laughed. When he stopped laughing he responded.

"Your Highness is a lovely woman. She should have those meetings nightly."

"Did you just make a pass at me Captain?"

"No, Your Highness, I mean, not really, I mean......
frack!"

"Tamika, relax. I may be a Princess in title, but I had a Centaurian Lancer Mother, remember?"

"Yes, and the stories I've heard about your Mother, outside the bedroom of course."

"Of Course."

"If I may be excused Your Highness, I shall see your instructions are carried out immediately."

"Captain, one last thing. Have the Lancers clean out my Fleet apartment and package everything for shipment. I have the feeling going back to Denoyelles may be a risk we should not take at the moment."

"As you command, Your Highness."

He bowed his head deeply and stepped back, before turning away from her. He made a signal with his hand and the doors opened, allowing another Ambassador to enter.

By the end of the day, she had met with over twenty Ambassadors except the ones from Hanover and the Federation. She had figured they would be some of the first to extend their greetings, but the question in her mind was why they were not present.

As she was having dinner with Sabella in your apartment, first there was a knock on the door, then it opened to allow Captain Gannaway access. He walked to the table and bowed his head before speaking.

"Your Highness, I have come to advise you that your things have been packed and loaded onto an assault boat. Where do you wish them to be shipped, My Lady?"

"Captain Gannaway, are you going to persist in the usage of Royal terminology every time you speak to me?

"Your Highness, I am but a servant."

Jilena exploded out of her chair and drew so close to him her breasts were pressing against his equipment vest.

"Mister Gannaway, the next time you utter such words to me concerning your position in life, I will personally strip you of your lovely fur, hair by hair while pouring alcohol into the open pores. You are not, and never will be a servant to me, or another as long as I live, is that understood?"

"Yes, Ma'am."

"Remember that too. Now, have you eaten?"

"No, Ma'am."

"Then sit your ass down and have something with us. Damn kitchen thinks I can eat for four."

She stepped back to her chair and looked at his face. No fear but puzzlement.

"Sit Tamika and talk with me. This is Sabella, my Yeoman. In my quarters or where it is private, please, call me Commander if you must use a title. It is one I am more familiar with than Your Highness."

"Thank you, but please let Uncle Ismael know of your instructions, because he'll rip my fur out by the handfuls if he thought for a second I was being disrespectful."

Jilena laughed as he smiled then chuckled.

"Sit Captain and we'll decide what to do with my meager belongings."

Gannaway only had a bit of fruit and a small glass of wine as he advised Jilena of what information he had on the two failed assassins and what to do with her belongings. He told a couple of stories about Ismael and she told of the ones she knew before he asked to be excused to return to his duties.

After Gannaway left, Sabella spoke up.

"That Captain is a handsome man. I hear that the fur of a Centaurian is very erotic when it touches bare flesh."

"Well Sabella, Lancer line officers are not married, so if you have the chance, have a go at Captain Gannaway. And yes, it is very erotic, sensual."

"Oh, I doubt I'll have a chance with the Captain."

"Why's that Sabella?"

"Commander didn't you notice? If you had thrown your dress up and laid back on this table, he would have taken you right here with me enjoying my pudding."

"Sabella, I think you may need your eyes examined."

"Really Commander, then why did you ask him to sit down with us?" Sabella had a sly smile on her face.

"Sabella, I think I may have to transfer you to waste management."

"If that pleases you Commander, I shall go without hesitation."

"Damn you Sabella. You know I would never do that. Besides, that would be cruel to the men who work down there."

Sabella laughed as did Jilena.

Later that evening, Jilena was able to talk to her Grandmother without Sabella present.

"Grandmother, I am lost here."

"How so Jilena?"

"I was never trained to rule a single world, now I have two of them to concern myself with. I never should have let Ismael talk me into this."

"Granddaughter, Ismael only told you what you needed to hear for you to make your own decision. He is a sneaky rascal for sure, but he would not have said whatever he said to convince you unless it was good for either you or those you will affect. Like a true Centaurian, yes, he will sacrifice all that he loves for others, including you. But there had to be truth to what he said, otherwise he would not have said it."

"I suppose you are right. Grandmother I'm concerned about Mother and Father, my brothers and sisters and of course my step-mothers."

"Jilena, your family is being protected. Your siblings have been told to request asylum at the Hayutan Embassy's and those in the Fleet are under protection. Lancer protection where possible, and Centaurian Marines where possible. It's the best we can do under short notice. Have you heard from the Federation yet?"

"No Grandmother and that bothers me."

"Jilena, you have served enough time to be legally able to surrender your commission, resign from the Fleet without them forcing you back into the service as a crew member."

"Yes, I am aware of that Grandmother. But I have a question to ask you and please, be honest with me. Are you behind me assuming the thrones?"

"Jilena, do I have my fingers in this, yes. I cannot now and maybe never explain to you why, but if you have every trusted me, trust me now. The Hayutan Council allowed me to renounce the throne but never allowed me to completely step aside, regardless how things looked. Even now they stay in contact with me, but I can now refuse them as I do more to support you. My dearest Jilena, you are the Throne of Hayuta and Bellus. Within days, my father will announce that you are the Protector of Keres as he is tired and wishes to retire."

"How can I rule over three world systems spread apart over nearly half the known universe?"

"Granddaughter, when I wrote the Principles of Leadership for Hayuta, I used our ancestors writings to do so, only I purified them a bit. Count Conrad made several mistakes and he allowed several voids which has allowed the Federation to slowly creep back into what it once was. Place your realm under the Principles and make the reality of failing to follow them all too real. They are yours to rule in such a manner and in doing so, you will find you will have more than enough time to enjoy the fruits of your labors. You'll have time to enjoy life without burden."

"Until then?"

"Until then, be strong. Surround yourself with those you trust. And Jilena. If love passes your way, grab hold of it and hang on."

"Now that's an odd comment Grandmother."

"Yes, it is, but remember how I met your Grandfather. Now it's late there, so go, rest and take tomorrow as it comes to you."

"Thank you, Grandmother. Give my love to Grandfather. Good night."

Jilena sat in the dark for over an hour, sipping on a glass of wine thinking about what her Grandmother had told her. First Popkyn, now Grandmother. What is not being told to her which may help her and keep her alive.

The Principles of Leadership were solid concepts and Hayuta worked hard to maintain them. Grandmother Lujayn recognized the weakness within mankind and used the Principles to counteract those weaknesses.

Yes, she would set those Principles over the people of Bellus, but she wanted to wait, if possible, until Lord Mikhail retires and hands over the Protectorate to her.

Jilena went to bed wondering what tomorrow would bring her.

It was ten the next morning that the play she was expecting was made. Her first appointment was not only with the Ambassador from Hanover but included a representative from the Federation Congress. It was the Federation representative that asked a question she actually never suspected to be asked.

"You Highness, Princess Jilena, since you are now next in line to the Throne of Denoyelles, will you reinstate the Hanover Throne?"

"Representative Munger, as I understand it, the Hanover Throne resides under the Dukedom of Denoyelles, and only a Denoyelles can sit upon it. Duke Thomas could still have an heir, a direct heir to take the Dukes chair."

"Yes, Your Highness, but with the Throne of Bellus and Hayuta, you are now the second most powerful chair in the Federation, behind the Denoyelles dynasty. It is the concern of the Federation Congress of what your intentions are, Your Highness."

"Representative Munger, let me be honest with you. I do not know what I want for my midday meal today, so do not even think I know what I shall do about the Denoyelles throne since Duke Thomas is well and active. If he desires to consult with me, he will no doubt contact me which he has yet to do."

Jilena stepped around the table and moved within arm's reach of the Representative.

"But Mister Munger, the tone of your voice suggests you are trying to intimidate me. Do not think for a single moment that you have that ability. I have faced a female Liger protecting her cub and came out the victor. Go back to Congress and express this to them. Count Conrad laid down the principles by which the Universe should be governed. Tell Congress I expect my ancestor's principles to be upheld for the good of all people, not for the benefit of a few seeking power above their ability."

"Princess Jilena, you cannot threaten the Congress!"

"I've made no threat to Congress or the Federation. I have only expressed my feelings concerning what I have seen and heard since I assumed the Throne of Hayuta. I am Jilena Borland, descendant of Michael Denoyelles, a descendant of Count Conrad Denoyelles. If I make a threat, the Universe will know of it. Now leave and do as I ask, and if you ever enter these chambers again in an attempt to intimidate me, bring an army."

Jilena just turned away and walked to the back of the Throne Room and pushed aside a set of curtains then disappeared into the waiting room, then into the bathroom where she washed her face as she calmed down.

"Are you alright Commander?" Sabella had followed her into the bathroom.

"Yes Sabella, he just angered me with his condescending tone of righteousness. That man is a pig and he is lucky I was not wearing my swords as I might have gutted him like a pig."

"Commander, I was afraid you would strike him anyway."

"I came close Sabella, too close. Did you record my words to him?"

"Yes Ma'am."

"Go, send that recording to Duke Thomas so he will have it if he needs to defend me before Congress. I hate putting him in such a position, but when he declared me his heir, he put himself in such a position. Go, do as I ask please."

"Yes Commander."

That afternoon, Jilena had two surprises. The first almost rocked her back on her heels as Captain Gannaway escorted a robed Centaurian into the Throne Room wearing a sword on his hip. He approached the table but stopped back from it. The Centaurian was brown of fur with gray streaking through it showing his age. He dropped to one knee, drew his sword and held it above his head in both hands.

"Your Highness Princess Jilena of Hayuta and Bellus. I am Antanas Fechin, Envoy from the Council and Congress of Hawkings World or in the Hayutan name, Zyra. The people of Zyra pledge themselves to Your Highness."

Jilena looked at Gannaway who had a neutral look on his face as he looked straight ahead. She was schooled in the nature of such pledges and her actions in them. She stepped to the Envoy and with one hand, received the sword from the uplifted hands. Then she reached out and took one of his arms and spoke to him as she pulled at him to rise.

"Rise before me Lord Fechin, let no man or woman kneel before me as I am only human, not a God."

"Thank you My Lady Jilena."

"Lord Fechin, return to the people of Zyra and tell them I accept their pledge, but remind them they are a free people to govern themselves as I make no claim over them. If I find need of the people of Zyra, I shall remember this day and send out a call to them. Please tell the people I am honored to accept this sword as their pledge."

"I shall give the people your kind words your Highness. If I may be excused, I have a ship waiting to return me to Zyra." He unfastened the sword scabbard and handed it to her as he spoke.

"A moment please, I just had a thought. Lord Fechin, what is your function on Zyra?"

"I am Secretary to the Congress of Hawkings World, My Lady."

"Lord Fechin, I am in need of a Secretary to tend to my Throne, here on Bellus while I am off world. Would you consider taking such an endeavor?"

"Your Highness, I am but a simple Civil Servant who was given this great task today by special appointment of the Congress."

"Then Lord Fechin, if they trusted you to extend their wishes to me, then I feel I can trust you to represent me before the Council of Bellus in my absence. Will you honor me and accept that post?"

"My Lady Princess Jilena, it would be an honor to stand in your stead before the Council of Bellus."

"Then Lord Fechin, return to Zyra and express my thanks before Congress, collect what you desire to return with and do so as quickly as possible. Captain Gannaway will arrange security for you and quarters for you and your family."

"I have no family My Lady, I am a widower, and my children are all grown. My needs are simple."

"Captain Gannaway, see that his needs are met and then some, I cannot have my Secretary living in a broom closet."

"It shall be done Your Highness." Gannaway responded.

"Go Lord Fechin, when you return, we have work to be done."

"Yes, Your Highness."

Gannaway had a smile on his face and winked at Jilena. She took that wink as she had done something good. An hour later, Gannaway entered again, this time escorting a distinguished looking gentleman in civilian garb. The gentleman stopped short of the desk and bowed deeply from the waist before speaking.

"Your Royal Highness, I am Colonel Levi Delaney, and I am the Operations Officer for Lancer Headquarters on Hanover. May I have a few minutes of your time?"

Jilena looked at the Colonel then at Gannaway.

"Captain Gannaway, advise the Royal Guards I have a headache and I am not taking any more interviews today."

"Yes, Your Highness." He turned on his heel back to the doors.

"Colonel Delaney, please take a seat. Would you care for something to drink?"

"Your Highness, I'd like a tall glass of whisky, but I think either water or a nice fruit juice is best."

Jilena laughed as she sat down then he took his seat.

"Sabella, is there any of the fruit juice left over from our midday meal?"

"Yes, Princess Jilena, I shall go retrieve it. Two glasses?"

"Yes please. Now Colonel, what's on your mind?"

"First of all, Your Highness, we've hit a dead end with the two men who were going to plant a bomb in your quarters. They took a blind contract to plant a bomb in a specific apartment and were not aware who the target was until they saw your name on the door. But since that name is Donovan, they did not connect that name with your Highness."

"Damn, so that leads into a blind alley. Colonel, until I either resign or the Federation tosses me out of service, please, call me Commander. It's easier to say and softer on the nerves."

The Colonel laughed.

"Certainly Commander. Now the next thing is I have been sent here by Duke Thomas."

The Colonel took several papers from inside his jacket pocket. When he unfolded them Jilena could see they had a Royal Seal on them."

"Commander, all nine Regiments of the Lancers are under retainer to the Duke of Denoyelles. In a very real sense, we are his personal army if he so decides. Our current contract with the House of Denoyelles extends for the next twenty years. The Federation pays for our services at Embassies and work sites, but those are set on a monthly basis. And the Lancers can terminate those contracts without cause."

"Alright Colonel, what does that have to do with me?"

"Commander, here is the contract between the Lancers and the House of Denoyelles. Duke Thomas has signed the Lancers over to you for the remainder of our contract. He holds the Second Lancer Regiment in reserve for his own needs, but the rest are yours to command."

Jilena reached over and took the contract. She read each page carefully before sitting the documents on the table.

"Colonel as I understand, no Lancer unit can enter into combat on a world where the Lancers are already present in defense of that world?"

"Correct Commander."

"You already have a battalion of Keres, correct?"

"Yes Commander. They are attached to the Fleet units there to supplement that base."

"Send a second battalion to Keres for training. Also send one to Hawkings World."

He smiled.

"Bellus and Hayuta?"

"Of course, Colonel"

"Support units?"

"As you deem necessary Colonel."

"Commander, Duke Thomas has an aide, a Lancer who moves about in civilian clothes. He is our link to the Duke. May I suggest you also have such an aide?"

"You may, and if you do not mind, I would like Captain Gannaway as my aide since we have a mutual Uncle."

The Colonel laughed again.

"Commander, I was a Cadet Lieutenant when the Sergeant Major was a Corporal. More than once he saved my stupid ass, oh, pardon my language. But he saved my hide more than once before I learned how to properly lead men. And I had Senior Lieutenant Gannaway in my Battalion before I moved up. He's every bit his Uncle."

"That's good to know Colonel."

"Yes, well, one other thing. He will have to be promoted to Major as per Duke Thomas's requirements for his aide. I doubt if Gannaway will complain about the promotion, but he just might make some noise about being in plain clothes."

"Let him make all the noise he wants. Now how long will it take to start moving Lancers to the locations I desire?"

"As soon as I get to my assault boat, I'll send the execute commands with destinations. We, the Lancer Command, figured you would want to protect the Thrones and Keres. Hawkings was not considered but only a minor detail. We can move any battalion within hours of the order."

"Then do so Colonel, after you finish your glass of juice. And I'll let you break the news to Major Gannaway."

"Coward." He joked as he took a long drink of the cool fruit juice.

"I'm only half Centaurian Colonel. I know my limits."

It wasn't three minutes after the Colonel exited the Throne Room that Gannaway came storming into the room heading directly for Jilena. But instead of being at the table, she was sitting on the Throne, waiting for him. He stopped short of the first step to the Throne platform and just looked at her.

"Yes, Major, is there something you need to report?"

Jilena knew she had just poked him as she smiled at him, pretending not to know why he was before the Throne.

"What the hell are you thinking, Your Royal Highness?"

"In what are your referencing, Major Gannaway?"

"I'm talking about your appointment of myself as your Military Aide, My Princess."

"Oh that. Well, Colonel Delaney mentioned Duke Thomas has a military aide, and now that the contract for the Lancers is in my hands, I felt the need to also have an aide."

"You hold the contract?"

"Yes, Major, I do."

"Why me? I'm sure Colonel Delaney could have recommended several, more qualified officers than myself for the job as your aide."

"I'm sure he could have, but there is something they would not have that you do have, and that's my trust at the beginning. They would have to earn that trust where as you have not only done so, but we have ties that I feel insures that trust. Shall I go on?"

"No, My Lady, you do not need to go any further. So, if I screw up you contact Uncle Ismael and let him come and straighten me out, is that it?"

Jilena stood and stepped down to his level.

"No, Major Gannaway. You screw up and I just might take your head with the same blade I took the Liger's head."

She stepped closer to him and lowered her voice.

"Tamika, I'm scared of what I have found myself involved with. I need someone I trust to steady me without having to run to my parents or grandparents. If you are only half the man Ismael is, then I have made the right choice. I'm sorry if comparing you to Ismael upsets you, but it is the only measure I have in this."

"My Lady, I am never ashamed to be compared to the Sergeant Major. Alright Your Highness, I accept my new position with a caveat."

"And that is what Major?"

"My assignment is to advise you, not to make decisions for you. I will do my best to give you the most accurate information and advice possible, but it is on you to make the decisions. They rest purely on your head My Lady."

"I accept your caveat Major. Now go to the Royal tailor and have more suitable clothing made for your new assignment. Keep it business like and cut so you can wear your Plastron Armor under it along with a few things you may need to remove any threat to my person. You will also function as my personal bodyguard, which is how I will introduce you. Short of the bath and bed, you go where I go."

"I understand My Lady. Communications?"

"Yes, we should be able to do that without you having to lean over my shoulder. Arrange that please."

"It shall be done."

"Check with housekeeping for quarters as close to mine as possible. Oh, and Major have you made any friends since you arrived on Bellus. Friends you might wish to entertain in the evening? If so, hopefully I can give you time to enjoy their company."

"I have no attachments, friends, here on Bellus, nor back on Hanover. But if one finds my company desirable, I will let you know."

"Then go Major, make yourself ready for your new assignment. We'll have dinner at seven, so we can discuss your assignment further. We, being yourself and Sabella at my table."

Jilena turned away from Gannaway and went behind the Throne to the exits behind the curtains and walked the connecting passageway to the Royal Apartments. She went directly to the shower, stripped and took a cold shower before turning the heat up.

As she let the water run down her body she thought that she had just made a major mistake. She would have to watch herself very closely as being that close to Tamika she could smell the musky odor often given off by Centaurians and it began to excite her in a way she did not have time for, especially with one such as him.

Over the next week, Jilena spent her free time studying the Principals of Leadership her Grandmother wrote for Hayuta. She presented them to the Council of Bellus, who in it's infancy, had copied the Federation Charter written by Count Conrad. She spoke in length to the Council about the gaps which were mistakenly left in the Charter which were being exploited by groups within the Federation to exert power over lesser worlds striving to grow.

She left the Principles with the Council to read and debate and after four days, they released them to the public as given to them for public debate. By the time Lord Fechin returned from Zyra, the public debate on the Principals moved to a demand for a vote. The people voted, casting almost ninety-seven percent for the Principals, with the votes coming in from the various Embassies echoing that percentage.

Within hours of Bellus accepting the Principals, the Federation issued orders for Jilena to return to her Fleet duties on Denoyelles. She was about to write out her resignation when she received a message from Keres. Lord Mikhail requested her presences on Keres, and she was not to resign until he spoke with her. Lord Mikhail apparently knew of her orders to return to Denoyelles.

Lord Garrick reported that he was receiving messages from all over the Federation advising her not to return to Denoyelles as there was fear for her life. Jilena told him to express her thanks to all that had communicated with him, but if she hid behind a wall of Marines and Lancers, what measure of freedom would she be expressing to the people she was honored to serve as their leader.

Gannaway also expressed his concern for her safety, even with Lancers at her side. Her response only made him nod his understanding of her position.

"Major Gannaway, somehow I have become to pillar of freedom within the Federation. My ancestor Count Conrad stood alone as he challenged the old Federation and the corruption within it. For eons, the powerful have sent out men and women to do their bidding while hiding behind a defended wall. I will not go down in history as one of those. If I have to send those out to fight the battles I am not capable of, then I shall not hide behind them, but stand firm in front of those who would see me dead to propagate their own selfish causes."

Keres

Jilena lifted to the Wyatt in the middle of the night in a similar manner in which she landed. She stripped out of her uniform and went to the toilet of her stateroom to relieve her bladder. As she stepped out of the bath, drying her hands, she found herself looking at Gannaway as he was standing inside her stateroom.

Gannaway looked at Jilena only dressed in her thin panties and bra as she exited her bathroom. When he realized he was staring at her, he quickly turned his back on her before speaking.

"Forgive me My Lady. I knocked and thought I heard you tell me to enter. I shall not make that mistake again."

"I did not hear your knock, Major. Please ask Ship's Maintenance to put a buzzer on my door during the next day cycle so I can hear someone while in the bathroom. Besides you have seen females in their underwear."

"Yes, My Lady I have, but you are not just any female. Forgive me please."

"If the sight of my body offends you, let me put a robe on then you can complete your mission which brought you here."

"Thank You, My Lady."

She put her robe on then sat down on the edge of her large bed.

"What brings you here, Tamika?"

"Commander, the Fleet knows you are headed to Keres. Word is they will instruct Fleet Sector Headquarters, Keres to not give you clearance to land and if you do land, to arrest you for disobeying orders to return to Denoyelles."

85

"Do you have any word from Keres concerning those orders?"

"Only silence Commander."

"Very well. We have three days to consider our actions upon arriving at Keres. Thank you and get some rest, you look tired."

"Thank you, My Lady."

He started out the door and stopped, speaking without looking at her.

"My Lady Jilena, I was not offended by your body. Just the opposite."

He stepped through the door without waiting for a response as Jilena just smiled thinking one day it will happen, but not this day nor tomorrow. It will happen because if not, they will both explode from the inability to release the desires they both feel. She turned in for the night and thought for a moment before sleep took her. It was not love but sexual desire they were feeling. Pure animal desire to couple and enjoy each other.

The next three days was taken up with communications with her parents and grandparents getting their advice on how to handle any situation with the Fleet. But it still came down to her own decisions concerning her actions. She knew that Lord Mikhail, her Great-Grandfather, was planning to turn over the Protectorate to her upon arrival at Keres.

Jilena was in Combat with Gannaway listening to the helm on the Bridge talk to Keres approach as they entered the planetary system. Fleet control entered the control net and advised the Wyatt not to enter into orbit. Keres Control was abrupt and told Fleet Control to stay off their net, and any attempt to interfere with the Wyatt attaining orbit would be dealt with by the Lord Protector.

Gannaway had a grin on his face as he leaned over to Jilena.

"My Lady, the Twenty-Second Lancers, the ones you sent to support the Eighth has moved into position on the Destros Space Port, and they have not done so in stealth. The Fleet is aware of their presences. The Eighth is active in patrolling the port, and the Fleet Marines have retired to their barracks. You may land without worry, My Lady."

"Once in orbit, we'll go directly to Lord Mikhail's home. A single assault boat and we'll land on his private pad. Any problem with that idea Major?"

"No, My Lady, but I see it as a slap in the face of the Fleet."

"No, if I am slapping anyone, it is the jackasses that issued the orders to Destros. And if I am asked, that is how I shall frame my thoughts on the matter."

"Makes sense to me My Lady. What now?"

"Pack a bag for a couple days for our stay at Lord Mikhail's home. He has more than enough room for myself, you and Sabella. Advise the Twenty-Second they are to provide security around Lord Mikhail's while I am there, and that the Eighth is to take over such security after I leave. That should shake the Fleet up a bit."

Gannaway chuckled without responding.

There was no interference in deorbiting an assault boat or landing on Lord Mikhail's private pad. The Lancers of her Security Detail now wore scarlet berets to set them apart from other Lancers, and had their helmets also painted scarlet.

Lord Mikhail met Jilena at the gate to the back of the house and she was amazed in that at age ninety-three, he was fit and agile. She bowed to him, then closed to hug and kiss his cheek before introducing Gannaway and Sabella. Lady Pilar was at his side and gave Gannaway an odd look.

Inside the house, Lady Pilar introduced her sisters, the other wives of Lord Mikhail to Gannaway and Sabella, then showed them their rooms for the duration of the stay while Jilena went into Mikhail's office for a private conversation.

As Pilar was showing Gannaway his room and facilities, she was asking him questions which he felt was odd in nature but had heard Pilar was not like other women. When she asked her last question, she nodded twice then touched Gannaway on the side of his face and smiled at him.

"Yes, Major Gannaway, you'll do, but it is you which must take the step."

She left him in the middle of his room puzzled by her questions and statement. He put his things away then went into the main room to wait until Jilena was finished with her private conversation with Lord Mikhail.

"Jilena, I wish it was your Father who was sitting with me today, but it must be you. When I say I'd prefer your Father it has nothing to do with your sex, but it's because you have enough to deal with as it is. I'm sorry to place this burden on you, but it must be done."

"Honored Ancestor, I have come to understand I am a victim of the Universe's bad timing. All I can do is shoulder the burden and pray I do not drop anything."

"Granddaughter, I never wanted the title the people of Keres gave me decades ago, and for the most part, once peace came to Keres, it has been almost no burden at all. But have you noticed that once you take over from me, you will have at your fingertips over a third of the known Universe, and from what I hear, that will grow in time. The worlds inside the arch of worlds that are at your disposal will flock to you for protection, and with them comes their planetary fleets and militia's. Use them wisely."

They talked for almost an hour before there was a knock on the office door. Gannaway entered.

"Lord Mikhail, there is a delegation of Keresan's here Sire."

"Good, it is time Jilena. We cannot wait any longer."

"I'm not ready for this Honored Grandfather, but I shall accept my fate."

In the main room of the house, a delegation representing the three main cities of Keres was present. They were the leaders of the World who looked to Lord Mikhail for protection and guidance. Ten minutes after Jilena entered the room behind Mikhail, she was declared The Protector of Keres.

Less than an hour later they had another group of visitors, this time from the Fleet. As before, the meeting was held in the main room with Gannaway beside Jilena in case he needed to protect her. It was not lost on the Fleet officers that both Jilena and Gannaway were wearing swords.

"Lieutenant Commander Donovan, I am Commodore Cuddihy, Fleet Commander of the Keres Sector. I have been instructed by Fleet Headquarters, Denoyelles, to advise you that you are in violation of Fleet Orders directing your return to Denoyelles for reassignment. I have been instructed to place you under arrest, and to return you to Denoyelles by the fastest transport I have available."

He never paused for a response but bowed deeply as his waist.

"Your Royal Highness, Princess Jilena Borland, the Keres Sector Fleet and Marines are at your command."

"Commodore Cuddihy, you are aware you have just committed treason and have violated your Fleet oath."

"Your Highness, I must follow my conscious in this matter. I believe there is a disease within the Federation and if you are not the cure, then all is lost anyway. Your ancestor Lord Michael choose treason over the Federation when he quarantined Bellus. His reasons have never been completely explained, but we are all the better for it."

"Commodore, have you polled the men and women of the Keres Fleet on their feelings? Any member of the Fleet that does not wish to stand with me, let them return to Denoyelles, unhindered and with dignity."

"It shall be so Your Highness."

"With those left, continue to patrol, protect the sector the best you can, if you need assistance, contact Hayuta for additional ships and personal. Yeoman Sabella, insure the Hayutan Council receives my instructions to the Commodore and my promise of support."

"Yes, My Lady."

"Is there anything else Commodore?"

"No, Your Highness, except to ask that you transmit your resignation from the Fleet as soon as possible. Once that is done, then the Fleet is exempt from any attempts to remove you from your position and return you to Denoyelles."

"It shall be done within the hour Commodore with a copy to your Headquarters."

"Thank you, Your Highness. We shall try to see that your visit to Keres is a peaceful one. By your leave, My Lady."

Jilena just stood, watching the Fleet officers as they left thinking something still was not right, and she felt it was her more than anything.

"How have I missed this rot that seems to be permeating the universe? She spoke to no specific person.

"You're an engineer Jilena, you think in clear terms unlike politics which maneuvers in the shadows. It's often hard to see the decay in a foundation even if you know it's there. With people it is often even harder." Her grandfather replied.

As she turned, she stumbled and was caught by Gannaway before she could fall. He had just reached out to catch her and in doing so found his hand grasping one of her breasts as he pulled her close to steady her. Gannaway just held her for a moment or two before she spoke.

"Thank you, Tamika, I have my footing now."

"My apologizes for how I held you My Lady." He spoke as he released her.

"That's alright, Tamika, my breast just got in the way."

Neither said another word as she left the main room and went back to her bedroom where she laid down still feeling the heat of his hand on her thinking how nice it felt even as awkward as the situation was. She fell asleep until Sabella woke her for the evening meal.

For three days, Jilena sat in Lord Mikhail's office working on whatever Sabella laid in front of her from Hayuta, Bellus and even Zyra, plus going over her notes from her inspection tour. Gannaway kept her appraised of the military aspect of events beginning to unfold within the Federation.

Her communications with the Councils of Bellus and Hayuta were set up for an hour each session with an hour between Bellus and Hayuta so she would not be overwhelmed. Everyone

91

within the house tried to make her life as easy as possible, but with world governments petitioning Bellus and Hayuta to join in an alliance, and the Councils of both worlds seeking guidance from the Throne, she was becoming worn out. Her advice was to always fall back on the Principles of Leadership to determine if such an alliance was practical and just.

It was Pilar, Jilena's Great-Grandmother that finally had to put the brakes on the situation. But her method was not what anyone could have imagined as she made her suggestion over the evening meal.

"Jilena, have you considered building your headquarters, your own palace if you will, here on Keres? It places you nearly equal distance between Hayuta and Bellus and you have an abundance of land for doing so."

"No, Grandmother Pilar, I have not had time to consider such a thing."

"Well, let me make a suggestion then. We have a mountain retreat which, although small, could be a starting point for such an idea. The air is fresh, and there is not too much snow even in the winter season. Take a couple of days, look at the area and consider it. This will accomplish several things."

"What's that Grandmother?"

"For one you get a couple of days away from that desk. The Councils keep coming to you for answers they already have, force them to act in your stead based upon your previous guidance. Then by taking a couple of days, Sabella here can get some time with Iseul's grandson, Corbin, which I believe she would greatly enjoy."

Sabella nearly choked on the drink of juice she was taking when her name was spoken.

"Sabella, are you and Corbin keeping company after hours?" Jilena asked her.

"My Lady, we have gone to a play and a pub in Sunow, but that is all."

Jilena, sat for a minute thinking about how long their hours had been.

"Tamika, and you?"

"Princess, Lady Pilar is right. You are doing the Council's work for them. You are tired and that can lead to a mistake which can have nasty effects if one is not careful. We are well protected here on Keres and time away from the desk would do you good."

"Tamika, I meant do you have someone to spend the time with while off?"

Gannaway looked at Pilar remembering what she had said about him having to make the move, take the step.

"Yes, Princess, but she has been too busy to notice me."

Jilena looked at Gannaway as she picked up her glass then took a long drink from it.

"Sabella, after dinner, please send a message to anyone that might require it. I am taking four days away from my duties to rest, and unless someone declares war, I do not wish to be bothered. They have the Principals to guide them, use them in good faith."

"It shall be done Princess."

The next morning, Gannaway piloted the aircar with just Jilena in it to the mountain retreat. It was smaller than Lord Mikhail's Sunow home since it was only meant for a single couple, not a brood or even all three of his wives at the same time. The caretaker was there stocking the pantry and left for his own cottage over a kilometer away.

Jilena walked the grounds, looking out over the distant valley and thought about how peaceful it was. She looked around and realized she was all alone, Tamika was not by her side or behind her as he had been since she appointed him as her aide. For the first time since being stranded on a new world, she was alone and it both frightened her and at the same time seemed to refresh her.

She had no idea how long she stood there, looking out over the valley until she seemed to sense he was once again behind her. Jilena turned to see him just standing there, looking at her without speaking.

"Tamika, this is beautiful."

"Yes, Princess, it is."

He stepped close to her, took her in his arms and pulled her close and kissed her. Jilena's response was one of surrender and acceptance as she returned his kiss with her arms going around his neck. When they final broke the kiss, they just looked at each other for a moment before he spoke to her.

"Forgive me Princess, I was caught up in the beauty of you and the view of the valley."

"Then why are you still holding me Tamika?"

"Because I want to kiss you again."

"What's stopping you?"

Instead of kissing her, he scooped her up and carried her into the house, and into the bedroom.

They spent their days walking the mountain, looking for a site to build her palace, but one that would not distract from the beauty of the mountains. Their nights were long and sweaty as they learned about each other in a carnal way as neither seemed to have their thirst for one another filled, but the drinks they were taking were more than satisfying.

Jilena began drafting what her mountain home would look like before she left the mountain. Tamika added a few things to her concept for security reasons and she incorporated them into her design.

As they were loading their bags in the aircar to return, Jilena told Tamika to move into her room with her. She wanted the comfort of his body next to hers as she slept once the day was done.

Fires

Between her Royal duties, Jilena drafted prints for her estate on the mountain. She showed them to anyone who might give her a better idea before finalizing them. Tamika requested Lancer Engineers for the heavy work of preparing the ground and special work needed, but Jilena asked for craftsmen from Keres to do the construction and interior of the estate.

As this was happening, the Federation Congress was taking steps to stop the growing dissention within the Federation by actually making it harder for worlds to enter into trade alliances without Federation approval.

When it was noted that exotic woods from the rain forests on Denoyelles were to be shipped to Keres for Jilena's estate, the Federation attempted to stop the shipment. Duke Thomas got around their phony tariff restrictions by having the materials loaded on a Lancer Support freighter. No Fleet officer would dare to stop a Lancer ship and board it for inspection.

Things between Jilena and Tamika often became strained during the day, as he would give her advice she often did not wish to hear. He maintained his position as her military aide and told her often advice from others can be painful, especially if the advice is given in complete honesty. His function was to be as truthful as possible without regard to her feelings on the matter otherwise his position was no longer a viable one.

Jilena's step-Grandmother Iseul told them both over dinner soon after their return that the troubles of duty should never cross the threshold of the bedroom. Duty was one thing, but love lasts long after duty ends.

A month after they became lovers, Jilena performed a Centaurian bonding ceremony in the main room of Lord Mikhail's home. She went on both knees in from of Tamika and offered her sword to him as acceptance of him as her mate, her husband.

Before he accepted her sword, he made a condition to their bonding.

"Jilena Kaylani Borland, if I accept this bonding I do so with the understanding that your Royal duties to the people who have placed their trust in you comes before all other things, including my own happiness. Until there is a time it can be otherwise, you are first my Princess, then my wife. A wife who stands beside her husband, not a servant to him. Do you accept my conditions, My Princess?"

"I do."

He took her sword as required in the ceremony and held it as she rose, then handed it back to her as a sign of their equality. She then had him kneel and christened him Lord Tamika Gannaway, Royal consort to the Thrones of Bellus and Hayuta.

It was during the small celebration afterwards that Pilar was able to quietly as Jilena a question.

"Are you with child, Jilena?"

"I've not seen a doctor as you know time has gotten away from me, but I believe I am."

"Tomorrow we shall go into Sunow, see our physician and have the test done. Until then, enjoy your wedding night."

The next morning it was confirmed, Jilena was with child but it was too early to determine sex of the child. When she returned home, her good news was tempered by the news Tamika had waiting for her.

"Princess, there has been an incident."

"Explain it to me Tamika."

"An independent freighter out of Lagos, was intercepted two days from orbit on New Holland with a cargo of farm equipment by a destroyer out of New Earth. It was not a Fleet destroyer but one of New Earth's Planetary Defense ships. The crew was arrested, and the ship confiscated under a new tariff law passed by the Federation Congress three days ago. That tariff law states that trade must be conducted within each sector unless approved by the Federation Office of Trades. The farm equipment was bought from a firm on Braxton, outside the New England/New Holland sector."

"Sabella, do I have an Embassy on New Holland?"

"Let me look Princess." A minute later she continued. "No Princess, but you do have a Consulate."

"Why does New Earth ring a bell?" Jilena asked no one in particular.

"Princess, your survey report pointed out a discrepancy in payments to a construction company on New Earth."

"Yes, I wonder. Sabella, connect me to the Consulate on New Holland."

"Princess, it may not be a secure link?"

"Good. This might be better that way."

"Yes Princess."

As Sabella arranged the communications link with New Holland, Jilena pulled up her report and found the paragraph Sabella mentioned. She wondered if there was a connection.

"Princess I have a connection."

"Thank you, Sabella."

Jilena stepped in front of the holographic projector. She could see a balding man on the other end.

"Sir, do you recognize me?"

"Yes, Your Highness. You are Princess Jilena, the Throne of Bellus."

"And you are Sir?"

"I am Simon Ronson, Consulate General to New Holland from Bellus. What service may I perform for your Highness?"

"You are aware of the freighter hauling farm equipment from Braxton being stopped and boarded?"

"Yes, Your Highness, I am."

"Is the need of that equipment critical to the farmers on New Holland?"

"Yes, Your Highness, it is. The planting season is almost upon us and that equipment was financed by a group of farmers and businessmen to build up the farms on New Holland. Without it, several farms may go under, and the planet may face a food shortage."

"How familiar are you with the purchasing of this equipment?"

"I'm not well versed My Lady. But as I understand it, the only world within the sector with such production facilities for this equipment wanted over twice what Braxton offered it for."

"Where is that facility located?"

"New Earth, Ma'am."

"Why do I suspect that if the people of New Holland has to import food for its people, it will come either from New Earth, or through New Earth brokers."

"Yes, Your Highness, according to the new tariffs, that's how it will have to be purchased."

"Mister Ronson, I think you for your time. Please advise the principles on New Holland that the Throne of Bellus has taken an interest in their problems and will examine those problems to see if the Throne can assist them."

"I shall immediately Your Highness."

Jilena signaled for Sabella to break the connection.

"Princess, what are you thinking?" Tamika inquired.

"I'm thinking that New Earth destroyer was in position to intercept that shipment before that new tariff was passed. I'm thinking a lot of the Federations problems begin with New Earth."

"And?"

"Sabella, if I remember correctly, each cargo manifest is listed with the Fleet and is public by freighter. See if you can locate the manifest for the freighter New Earth confiscated."

"Tamika, we have a Lancer support freighter here on Keres, right?"

"Yes, Princess."

"Have it emptied, place two sections of Lancers on board and send it to Bellus. Hopefully before it gets there I will have a complete plan. Do it now Tamika, time is important."

"Yes, Princess."

Jilena went to the holographic projector's computer and displayed a holographic image of the Federation. It indicated where she was on Keres, and she then asked for the New Earth sector to be highlighted. She entered the projection and she touched the image of a planet, it's information was displayed beside it.

"Princess, I have the manifest."

"Value of cargo?"

"Twelve million Crowns, delivered Princess."

"Bring my cubes in. I need to talk to Lord Garrick and if need be Lord Popkyn on Hayuta."

It was nearly ten minutes before Lord Garrick appeared above the crystal communicator.

"Yes, Your Highness?"

"Lord Garrick, I never inquired to my wealth, the wealth of the Throne which I hope is separate of the planetary wealth, but can I afford, oh say, twenty million Crowns?"

"Your Highness, that will barely be noticed."

"Thank you. Sabella will send you a cargo manifest from the freighter New Earth stopped and confiscated. I am sending a Lancer Support Freighter to Bellus. Match or better that manifest with new equipment from our factories on Bellus. The invoice will be made out to Simon Ronson, Ambassador to New Holland. Note I said Ambassador, see that his appointment is made within the hour. The equipment will be loaded on the Lancer freighter as quickly as possible, so they can transit to New Holland. I guarantee payment for the equipment out of my personal funds."

"Your Highness what you request will be done. The equipment should be waiting for the freighter when it arrives. And I will see to Mister Ronson's appointment in the meantime."

"Advise Ambassador Ronson to find quarters for a section of Lancers who will provide security for the Embassy and if he needs larger facilities for an Embassy, to do so while he waits for the shipment to arrive."

"Yes, Your Highness."

"Edon, in two hours, return as I wish to speak to you and Hayuta together."

"Yes, Your Highness."

When the connection was broken, she continued to examine the holographic image of the Federation.

"What's on your mind Princess?" Tamika asked.

"You once told me that as an Infantry officer you often had to think like an engineer. How to construct defenses when needed, and how to overcome defenses in the attack. The first shots of a civil war have just been fired, I intend to put the fires out before bloodshed can be brought."

"Alright, how do you propose to do that?"

"Tamika, right now, I am going to lie down and think. Make sure I am up in time to be wide awake to talk to Bellus and Hayuta."

"Sabella, contact Lord Popkyn and inform him to have President Claiborne present at the time I indicated, and advise him it will be a joint call with Bellus."

"Yes Princess."

Tamika followed Jilena to their bedroom and after she laid down, he kneeled down by the bed and laid his head on her stomach.

"Jilena was this intended or a pleasant accident?"

"Are you talking about the child that is growing in me My Love?"

"Yes, My Princess."

"It is a very pleasant accident. I would have liked waiting until all these troubles were past, but one cannot argue with fate."

"Take care of yourself My Princess, fore I doubt my life would have any meaning without you."

"I shall My Love, now let me rest, there is much to do later."

As she rested, the heads of the governments of Hayuta and Bellus communicated and decided to hold the meeting with the entire Councils present to insure they followed her instructions. This surprised Jilena, but she thought they had made the right decision considering the position she was putting the World's in.

"Councils, thank you for joining with me today, especially the Hayutans who for them, this is the middle of the night. Now first of all I would like the Hayutan communications specialists set up a secure system between Hayuta and Bellus along in preparing one for the home I am building here on Keres. Keres is close to being equal distance between both Thrones and my establishing a Throne here would make it easier for me to travel from world to world when it is required. I am open to debate on this as per the Principals of Leadership."

She could see several people put their heads together on Hayuta, and a couple exchange comments on Bellus but no one spoke up about her decision.

"Thank you, and the debate can be opened at any time. Now, I have news of importance. Yesterday in a private ceremony, I took Tamika Gannaway as my bond mate, my husband. I have christened him in ceremony as Lord Tamika."

"Excuse me Your Highness." This came from Garrick on Bellus.

"Yes, Lord Garrick?"

"When Princess Kaya married Michael Denoyelles, the Bellus Council deemed him Prince Michael." He turned to the Council. "How say you Council of Bellus?"

Jilena watched as each Council member gave a signal confirming Garrick's comments.

"Your Highness, the Council of Bellus recognizes Lord Tamika Gannaway as the Prince of Bellus."

Jilena motioned for Tamika to join her.

"We thank the Council of Bellus."

"Your Highness, the Hayutan Council echoes their approval and accepts Tamika Gannaway as Prince of Hayuta."

"I thank both Councils and will strive to do honor to the title both have given me this day." Tamika responded as he bowed his head in acceptance. He then moved out of the range of the projector, so she could continue.

"Lords and Ladies, one final note before we move on to the reason I arranged this meeting. I learned this morning, Keres time that I am with child."

Both Councils erupted in applause at the news. Jilena let it go on for a couple of minutes before she quieted them down.

"The sex of the child has yet to be determined, but I will advise the Councils once it has time to grow enough to make that determination. Now on to pressing matters."

Jilena explained her concerns about how the Federation was passing tariff laws in favor of one select group over another. She expressed her feelings based upon what evidence she had over the confiscation of the freighter headed for New Holland and her earlier instructions to Lord Garrick about replacing the confiscated equipment out of her own funds.

She went on for nearly thirty minutes explaining the meager evidence that they had developed and the results of her inspection survey. It was then that one of the Council of Bellus interrupted her.

"Your Highness, this might be a reach, but could your findings during the survey be linked to the attempt to kill you as you entered orbit around Bellus?"

"If it is Sir, that means there are factors far more sinister than the skimming of six million credits involved. Here is what I wish both Councils to do, independent of each other to insure accuracy."

She paused for a moment to collect her thoughts.

"Contact our Ambassadors on Hanover, and have them dig deep into the laws, regulations, and tariffs, to find any connection between them and New Earth. Then link those connections to the sponsors, and supporters of those bills. Let's see if we can develop a pattern of collusion, of violation of the Federation Charter. Do this quickly before another incident occurs which spills innocent blood."

"Your Highness." President Claiborne spoke.

"Yes, Lord Claiborne?"

"Have you contacted Duke Denoyelles concerning this matter?"

"No. I am concerned that if it becomes known he is investigating this, the principles involved with go to ground, begin to hide their involvements, making a case almost impossible to prosecute."

"Yes, Your Highness, I can see the validity of your statement. Hayuta will get right on your instructions, especially on the secure communications between Hayuta and Bellus. We can tie into your present location then move it as needed later so you are secure between us."

"Very good Lord Claiborne. Now unless someone has a comment or open the debate on my home here on Keres, I shall bid you are a fair day and close this off."

Jilena waited for over a minute before she broke the connections of her crystals to the Councils.

"My Princess, what are your plans now?" Tamika inquired.

Jilena stepped to Tamika and gently touched his face.

"My Love you are now a Prince, you no longer have to call me Princess?"

"Oh, but I do because you will always be My Princess." He replied with a grin.

She rose up and planted a light kiss to his lips.

"I think food is called for at this time, and I wish to pick my Grandmother's brain along with Lord Mikhail's. Then we shall see what develops from there."

Tamika requested communicators from the Lancers on Keres, so Sabella would not have to sleep with a communicator next to her bed and links could be quickly established. Especially since Sabella's love life seemed to be progressing with Corbin.

Lord Mikhail and his wives moved to the mountain retreat to they would not be underfoot and to be allowed their own privacy. Jilena promised to return his home to him as soon as her new palace was complete in the mountains, near his retreat.

Jilena instructed the communicators to use their best judgement concerning bothering her at night because even the most minor detail might be a clue to what they were searching for and she could always sleep in the next morning.

Two nights later, Jilena was awakened by a hard knocking on her door. She grabbed her robe and as Tamika sat up in bed, covering himself, she opened the door to find one of the communications techs standing in the passageway.

"My Lady, there is an urgent message from Bellus. It seems someone attacked the Embassy on New Holland during the night."

"Details?"

"The message is quite lengthy My Lady."

"Let me dress and I'll be right there. Would you fix a pot of tea please?"

"I have one already going My Lady, I was wanting a cup when the message came."

"Good. Thank you." She closed the door to see Tamika moving off the bed.

"Tamika, they moved quicker than I thought."

"Yes Princess, they have. This is good for us, bad for them."

"How is it good for us?"

"They are rushing things. That will cause them to make mistakes, and mistakes can be deadly. Get dressed as we don't have time for me to throw you back on the bed and make love to you."

Jilena laughed as she tossed off the robe and walked over to Tamika, pulled him close and kissed him. When she broke the kiss, he smacked her hard on her bare bottom causing her to yelp.

"Damn you woman, get dressed!" He spoke with a grin.

"Yes, Master Tamika, I shall Master Tamika. Damn that stung!"

When Jilena entered the bedroom that had been set up for communications, she found a thin stack of flimsies and a steaming cup of tea waiting for her. As she read each page, she passed it on to Tamika for him to read. By the time she finished, she was upset and just took her cooling cup of tea over to a chair, sat down and sipped on it waiting for Tamika to finish the report.

The attack had been crude, amateurish in execution but the one point that stood out was that the security of the consulate had seemed to disappear just before the attack then reappeared acting as if they were their all the time. Since this was a consulate instead of an Embassy at the time of its placement, security was contracted through a private firm on New Holland instead of utilizing Bellusarian Marines as was normal procedure.

Tamika laid the report back on the desk and looked at Jilena.

"What now Princess?"

"Contact the freighter and advise the Lancers they are to move on the Embassy, since that is what it is now, and take over security. I sent them to protect the shipment until it was in the hands of the farmers, but this is their new mission once that is accomplished. If additional Lancers are needed, get them moving."

"Yes Princess."

"Wait. Contact Colonel Delaney and find out what assets he has in that sector. Regardless of how security is being dealt with, I want Lancers at every Consulate and Embassy in the sector. This is for every post under my reign, including Hawkings."

"I'll get right on it Princess. Specialist, let's get a connection with Lancer HQ on Hanover, Colonel Delaney, please."

"Yes Sir."

Jilena sat and listened to the conversation between Tamika and Delaney once the connection was made. It wasn't until

Delaney mentioned New Earth that she became involved in the conversation.

"Colonel Delaney, did I hear you correctly that New Earth prohibits Lancers from protecting the Embassy's on their world?"

"Yes, My Lady. Up until about three years ago, we covered the Federation and Hanover Embassy's, then the regime on New Earth ordered them off."

"Interesting. Put those Lancers in my livery then. Let's see how they like that."

Delaney laughed. "Yes, My Lady, that should make things interesting. One other thing, Princess. According to what I see in front of me, Hawkings was restricted to fair skinned personal at their Embassy on New Earth. Personal such as Lord Tamika were prohibited because it was claimed they were a disruption amongst the people because of their unique appearance."

Jilena had to calm down before she responded to his statement.

"Colonel Delaney, that is in direct violation of Article Three of the Federation Charter. No person, regardless of race or creed will be prohibited from traveling or visiting another world unless they have been convicted of moral or capital crimes. Do you show any record of Hawkings protesting that rule on New Earth?"

"Yes, Princess. It was taken before the Federation Council and that rule was exempted for New Earth by a majority vote."

"Colonel Delaney. Instruct Lancer Intelligence to dig as deep as necessary into the dealings of the major players on New Earth. And I mean dig deep. Leave no stone unturned. Also have them locate the survey report I submitted to the Fleet just before I ascended the Throne of Bellus. Find every connection of those who might have read that report to New Earth."

"Princess, do you think the Fleet has been infiltrated?"

"It has happened before Colonel."

"Yes, it has. I will get Intelligence right on it. Now I must make this statement as per Lancer Charter. Your Highness, must be aware we are restricted to methods and techniques in developing Intelligence against Federation members in a non-combat environment."

"Colonel Delaney. I, Princess Jilena Borland, suspect treason and sedition against the Federation and instruct the Lancers to weed it out using whatever methods and techniques the Lancers feel is necessary to fulfill their mission. Does that cover the Lancers Charter?"

"Yes, Your Highness, it does."

"Colonel, then execute your instructions."

"Yes, Your Highness. As you command."

The link was broken as Jilena went over to the tea pot to refill her cup.

"Tamika, have I just started a war?"

"No Princess, you are only responding to another who seems to want a war, only your steps are less dangerous than theirs. I am surprised at one thing though."

"What's that Tamika?"

"That you did not order Centaurian Lancers to New England in spite of the restriction."

"I was tempted My Love, but that would have put those people in harm's way, making them a prime target. No, it was tempting but not logical."

"Princess, we have a message coming in from the Council of Bellus, My Lady."

"Print it off please."

"Yes, My Lady."

Jilena took each page as it was printed out and read it before once again passing it on to Tamika. The message was concerning the attack on New Holland and updated the previous message. Two staff members, along with the now Ambassador had been wounded but would recover. The Hayutan Embassy had sent a detail of Marines over to secure the area around the small Consulate building and had offered offices in their Embassy until a new facility could be moved into or built. The message ended with the Council standing by for further instructions.

"Specialist, advise the Council of Bellus that we are aware of the situation and have instructed the Lancers traveling with the farm equipment to assume the duties of protecting the Bellusarian Embassy once the farm equipment has been delivered. We are examining other options at this time. Tamika, do you think that is neutral enough at this time?"

"Sounds good to me My Princess. If anyone is reading our mail, then that should warn them we are not just rolling over for them. And it is not being aggressive either."

"Thank you, Tamika. Read that back to me Specialist."

Once it was read back, Jilena ordered it sent to include copies to the other Embassy's under her reign. Jilena returned to bed, and just snuggled with Tamika and hoped sleep would return before daylight.

But she had a restless night as she was concerned her actions were leading them into war. She knew the military status on New Earth which was no challenge to even the small Fleet of Keres, but who out there would join with New Earth?

How would the Federation Fleet react in such a situation? She already had the pledge from three Fleet Commodores, but she knew that unless the conditions were just right, she could not risk them committing treason just for her suspicions.

Sleep finally took her but awakening came too soon.

Waiting

Even with the improvements of engines reducing the time to travel from planet to planet from years to days, it still took time for the plans Jilena had set in motion to take effect.

One of the first effects was when the Lancers landed on New Earth wearing the livery of the Throne of Bellus and Hayuta. Even in that livery, the Lancers wore the Crossed Lances of the Lancers which caused the government of New Earth to file a protest with the Federation Council. New Earth wanted those personal removed immediately.

Jilena stood in the holographic projector as she listened to the President of the Federation Council read the protest from New Earth. She stood patiently until the President has finished and spoke before he could comment on the protest.

"Mister President, am I to understand that I am not allowed to provide protection to my Embassy's as accorded in Section Two of Article Five of the Federation Charter?"

"Your Highness, you have sent mercenaries onto a peaceful world."

"But Mister President, The Federation utilizes the Lancers to protect their own Embassy's all over the Federation. What does it matter if I do so, and besides, they are in the livery of the Throne, not in Lancer uniform."

"Your Highness, the government of New Earth views this as a threat to their sovereignty."

"Really now? Less than one hundred of my Royal Guards is a threat to their sovereignty? Is the military might of New Earth so weak they fear one hundred men and women whose only mission is to protect my Embassy's?"

"Your Highness, I don't know how to respond to that."

"Well Mister President, it is not my place to provide you with such answers, only questions needing answered."

"But Your Highness, this can cause a diplomatic incident?"

"If there has been an incident, it is because the government of New Earth did not contact the Throne to rectify the situation, and instead, contacted the Federation Council in protest. That again is in violation of the Federation Charter. Shall I go on, Mister President?"

"No, Your Highness, you have made your point quite well."

"Then I think we are done here."

Jilena made a motion with her hand which Sabella knew as to break the connection with the President.

"Tamika, I think I handled that very well, don't you?"

He laughed.

"Well, you certainly rocked him back on his heels. But My Princess, he will not be so uncertain the next time."

"Tamika, the only recourse to this situation at the Federation level is to rescind the Articles within the Charter. Which would basically cause the Federation to cease to exist. That would take one hundred percent of the Congress to agree upon by Charter. I have four votes that would say no, and no doubt Duke Thomas and his people would vote no, so where does that leave them?"

"In the middle of a very dangerous situation, My Princess."

"Yes, which I hope cooler heads will think before they act. Have we heard from Lancer Intelligence?"

"We received a report this morning. It seems large amounts of credits have been flowing from New Earth into

114

accounts all over the Federation, but who owns those accounts have yet to be discovered."

"If memory serves me correctly, Count Conrad was faced with the same problem when he confronted the old Federation. Corruption within the Federation caused its collapse, to be reborn again under his guidance and the Articles he wrote to prevent such a thing. Tell Intelligence to keep digging."

"I already have."

"Good, now I think a long, hot bath is called for."

She winked at Tamika who grinned knowing what she had in mind.

Each day, Jilena read reports coming in from Lancer Intelligence, showing that they were getting closer with each passing hour, but it was not enough to take to a Federation Court or to Congress.

The one thing she had to smile about was that her report had disappeared and within the hierarchy of the Federation Fleet Engineering department were two senior officers from New Earth. Had they seen the report and disposed of it before it went any higher? And why had no one from the Fleet asked why her survey report had not been filed?

Jilena had her report packaged and sent to Colonel Delaney with instructions to hand it off directly to the Admiral of the Fleet without comment. It was nearly thirty-six hours before she was contacted by the Admiral of the Fleet.

"Princess Jilena, I have read your report, and according to the time/date stamp on it, you properly filed it according to regulations, yet I cannot find it anywhere here at Fleet Headquarters. I take it that the manner in which this was delivered to me is an indication we here at Headquarters are not secure."

"Admiral Felix, that is what I suspect also."

115

"Your Highness, I am going to notate this as if I received it through normal channels and have finance look into the overcharges. This may not result in much, but it may shake a few rats out of the bushes. Without a record of who handled your report, there is no way I can call any officer in to discuss why it disappeared from our system."

"I understand Admiral. But it does give you something to consider. I hope the infection is not too wide spread."

"So, do I Princess. Again, thank you for bringing it to my attention."

Jilena hated the waiting part of what was happening, but there was nothing she could do about that except to patiently sit back and watch events as they occurred.

The Call

It had been a week since Jilena had talked with the Fleet Admiral and from the reports she was receiving, there were a lot of nervous people at Fleet Headquarters. Admiral Felix had restricted all Fleet Headquarters personal from off world flights until both Finance and the Inspector General's office could determine why are report from a Fleet Officer had disappeared without a trace.

Jilena was lying on a recliner on the back patio of the house dressed in the thinnest of panties and bra soaking up the morning sun when Tamika walked out of the house and stood so the sun would not be on her face.

"Woman, you certainly look enticing lying there like that."

She looked up at him.

"And you Sir, are rude, crude and wasting time. I figured you would have picked me up and carried me to bed by now."

He laughed.

"Maybe later but right now we have a communication from the Bellus Embassy on New Earth and it's interesting to say the least."

"What's it say?"

"At approximately 1630 hours, New Earth time, a group of thirty people gathered in the street in front of the Embassy and began to chant for the Lancers to go home. After about ten minutes of chanting, person or persons unknown began throwing over ripe vegetables at the two Lancer Sentries at the gates to the Embassy. It is reported that the Sentries just lowered their face shields and made no move to counter the assaults on their persons with the flying vegetables."

"Good for them, they should be commended for their actions."

117

"But it gets better My Princess. Approximately five minutes later, five Lancers exited the gates fully armed and ready for battle, but instead of turning weapons on the gathering, they brought with them baskets of apples which they began to hurl at the protestors. The protestors then moved away from the gate and crossed the street to continue chanting and throwing vegetables with several of the protestors bleeding from noses or split lips from being hit in the face by the much firmer apples."

Jilena began giggling at the thought of the Lancers returning fire with the apples.

"The protestors found themselves on the sidewalk in front of the Embassy of Danbury, whose security forces ordered the protestors to disperse. When the protestors refused and began hurling insults at the Danbury Security officer who order them to disperse, the Danbury Security forces withdrew behind their gates, then sprayed the protestors with a riot control irritant which also contains a semi-permanent dye, a bright purple dye. The protestors soon disperse under a hail of apples as they ran away."

By this time Jilena was no longer giggling but laughing out loud and holding herself to prevent her breasts from popping out of her bra. Tamika just stood and watched her as she enjoyed the image of the protestors being colored purple and chased away by the Lancers throwing apples at them. When she finally calmed down she asked what if any, the civil authorities had done.

"It seems they arrived as the crowd was dispersing and a couple of them were hit with the irritant. They made a feeble attempt to arrest the Lancers involved in throwing the apples for inciting a riot, but the Lancer Lieutenant in charge of security backed them down with video of the start of the confrontation. At no time was the Danbury Security personal questioned about their part in the incident."

"Of course not Tamika. They wanted an incident which they could use to have the Lancers removed from the planet. Please let the Lancers know the Throne appreciates their actions."

"I have already sent such a message. signed by His Royal Highness, Prince Tamika. If I have the title, I may as well use it."

"Yes you should My Prince."

"Now My Princess, off your ass and get dressed. You are starting to turn red in places that I do not want sunburned as I enjoy playing with them."

Jilena laughed and hopped up off the recliner, grabbed Tamika and kissed him hard before walking towards the house wiggling her rear as she heard him laughing at her.

They never made it to the bedroom as the Comm Tech on duty caught them in the passageway.

"Your Highness, we have a communications request from the Chancellor of New Earth."

"Have your responded yet?" Jilena asked.

"No, Your Highness."

"Good, reply back that I am away, inspecting the construction of my new mountain palace and you have messaged me and that I shall return within the hour and contact him. Then contact Hayuta and Bellus, you might add Zyra in on this to stand by to monitor the conversation. Once we can confirm everyone is ready, then we'll contact New Earth. Got that?"

"Yes, Your Highness."

"Good, go see to it. Tamika, no afternoon enjoyment just yet, but when everything is set up, you deal with the Chancellor."

"Princess My Love, it is obvious those New Earther's do not like us simple Centaurians. Is this wise?"

119

"Darling, what I wish is that you are firm, yet overly polite, which should bring out the worse in the Chancellor. And in doing so, we'll have a recording to take into court or before Congress showing how they are in violation of the Articles."

"Still building that foundation, are we?"

"If everything goes right, this conversation could be the reinforcing bar within the concrete. Wear your gray suit, it sets off that lovely fur coat of yours."

Tamika laughed as he followed Jilena into the bedroom. Not knowing how long it would take to up-link the other planets, they did not take advantage of being naked so close to a bed but did hold each other and kiss for a short time before they both dressed.

When the links were established with the Councils, Jilena explained what she hoped would be accomplished with this meeting as she had complete faith in Prince Tamika to express her desires and wishes in maintaining a diplomatic relationship with New Earth, but at the same time, if what she suspected was true, this meeting would expose the bigotry and bias of the New Earth government.

Tamika took center stage and indicated for Sabella to make the holographic connection between him and New Earth. The impact of seeing Tamika instead of Jilena was immediate. Tamika spoke first upon connecting.

"Good day Chancellor Lindhorst, what can the Throne of Bellus do for you this day?"

"I…...I was told I would be speaking to Princess Jilena, not some underling. Where is the Princess?"

"Well Chancellor that is a small problem. Princess Jilena is expecting a child as I'm sure you know and is not feeling well, so she asked me to deal with your problem. And as far as who I am, I am Prince Tamika, I stand beside the Throne of Bellus and Hayuta as husband to Princess Jilena."

"I demand to speak to Princess Jilena, not some Centaurian!"

"My goodness Chancellor Lindhorst, you really need to get control of yourself. I am not just some Centaurian, I am also the Military advisor to the Throne. Now please, relax and tell me what is so important that you feel I should cause the Princess to arise from her bed to speak to you."

It appeared that the Chancellor spoke to someone off to the side before further commenting.

"We demand you remove your mercenaries from New Earth immediately?"

"What mercenaries are you talking about Chancellor?"

"The Lancers that as posing as the Royal Guards at your Embassies!"

"Lord Chancellor, we have no mercenaries posing as guards, those individuals are sworn and certified members of Her Highnesses Royal Guard."

"Yes, so you say. And there are armed females in those guards!"

"Yes, Chancellor Lindhorst, they are there to provide support to any female diplomat or diplomats mate that visits those Embassies. We do not see that as a problem, only a matter of courtesy."

"But.... but they are armed!"

"They would be poor guards if they were unarmed, and they are highly qualified in those arms Chancellor."

"We want them removed!"

"Chancellor Lindhorst, we are within our rights under the Federation Charter and Articles to position those Guards at our Embassy's. And the incident earlier today only reinforces that decision."

"That's my point you beast, those guards caused that incident and injured several of my citizens in doing so!"

"Chancellor, we have video record of that incident from several angles to include footage from the Danbury Embassy that shows those protestors started throwing rotten vegetables at our Guards. To be honest, I applaud the Guards in their rebuttal by only returning fire with fruit instead of bullets. Tit for tat so to speak."

Everyone viewing the exchange could tell the Chancellor was becoming more and more frustrated with Tamika's soft tone and logical responses. Tamika decided to continue as the Chancellor seemed unable to find the words he was looking for.

"Chancellor, I'm not sure of the exact figures, but we have less than one hundred Royal Guards on New Earth. Are you afraid those small, but elite number of men and women will attempt to take over your world? Or are you afraid the next group we send to replace them will contain Centaurians such as myself? After all, Princess Jilena is half-Centaurian by her blessed mother."

"I demand you remove them immediately or else!"

"Or else what Chancellor Lindhorst?"

Before the Chancellor could speak again, the connection was broken from his end. Tamika stood waiting to see if it might be reconnected for several minutes then told Sabella to terminate the connection. He turned to look at Jilena.

"How did I do My Princess?"

"I think you did very well My Prince. Hayuta, your opinion?"

122

"Your Highness, the Chancellor is a scared little man who is also a bigot."

"Bellus?"

"We concur with Hayuta. But place notice that a person like him can be very dangerous if left unrestrained with his own madness."

"Zyra?"

"We must agree with previous comments. On a personal note, fifty thousand Centaurians walking on the streets of the Capital of New Earth would be a sight to behold. We salute Prince Tamika for not speaking about being called a beast."

"Thank you, Sir, but I'm a Lancer and have certainly been called worse."

That drew light laughter from all listening. Then Lord Garrick spoke up.

"Princess, what are your instructions?"

"Bellus and Zyra is to prepare one heavy cruiser each with a full complement of Marines and station them just outside of the New Earth Sector. They are to just float out there and if questioned about their presences, they are to only comment that they have been ordered there by the Throne and have no other instructions. If ask how long they would stay there, the answer is until ordered by the Throne to return to their home ports. Execute those orders immediately."

"Yes Your Highness." Echoed both Bellus and Zyra.

"What of Hayuta your Highness?" President Claiborne questioned.

"Is my Grandmother's project progressing as predicted?"

"We are ahead of schedule, My Lady."

"Has the modification of the Wyatt been completed?"

"Yes, My Lady, it has."

"Once you have a complement of Marines outfitted and on board the Wyatt, send it on to Keres. If I have to advance my plans ahead of the program, I can do so and allow the others to catch up."

"Yes, Your Highness."

"Sabella, break down the links please."

When they were alone, Tamika asked a question he had put off several times.

"Jilena, what kind of project do you have your Grandmother working on that is so secret that you have not even told me?"

"I'm sorry My Love that I have not confided in you on this. Grandmother is equipping a Hayutan Fleet and Marines with forbidden technology. Technology the Hayutans once used to move about the Universe while undetected until Grandmother ascended the Throne and took Hayuta into the Federation. If New Earth decides war is what they wish, then I can put six heavy Cruisers above their world plus a dozen smaller ships without them ever knowing it. I'll also put a brigade of Marines on the ground sight unseen."

"Cloaks? I thought that was just a myth?"

"No Tamika, they are not a myth. I even have one now, plus another for you. The Bellusarians had them when Prince Michael first discovered them, but he had all of that technology destroyed. Grandmother did not, she only hid it from prying eyes."

"A section of Lancers so equipped would be worth a company without. Is it wise to possibly expose the universe to such technology?"

"No, My Love, but I will use whatever tool I can lay my hands on to prevent a civil war. The people behind the curtains on New Earth only wish power and to shove their beliefs on the rest of the universe. If they think they can do this without a civil war, they have deceived themselves. As the Throne of the worlds I reign, I shall not allow this to happen as long as I have a breath in my body."

Two hours later they received a message from Duke Thomas.

"Ambassador from New Earth to the Federation recalled for consultation. Ambassador was injured before boarding shuttle when he 'tripped' over a Centaurian. Ambassador was hospitalized but is expected to recover in time. Two New Earth Fleet Officers arrested while trying to board a private yacht in violation of Fleet Orders. Status unknown. End of Message."

"Tamika, do you think Duke Thomas knows about the research the Lancers are doing?" Jilena asked.

"He's probably getting copies of what we are getting. Do you think Colonel Delaney would keep the Duke out of the loop on this?"

"No, and I cannot say I can be upset if he is. Alright, it's getting late, I want everyone to get some rest, tomorrow could be a very long day. Sabella, get to bed early tonight."

"My Lady, I have a date with Corbin tonight."

"That's what I said." Jilena replied with a smile.

As Jilena was issuing her orders for everyone to get some rest, Lancer Psych Doctors were walking through the minds of the two Fleet officers that were arrested in violation of orders. Fleet Admiral Felix had them turned over to the Lancers before any record of their arrest could be made to the Fleet Log and had informed Duke Thomas of his intentions and actions.

As far as Admiral Felix was concerned, those officers were traitors to their oaths based on the information he had on them and washed his hands of them.

A Failed Attempt

Two days later events took a dangerous turn when there was an attempt on Duke Thomas's life by a lone individual who tried to gain access to the Duke. The man was wearing a vest made of explosives and when he was able to force his way past the first barrier to the Duke and found he was trapped, he detonated the vest, killing himself and four others.

That same day Lancers that were protecting Jilena shot down an aircar that had been stolen as it tried to fly into the house loaded with explosives. The pilot was thrown out of the aircar before it crashed and exploded giving the Lancers a body to examine.

Video of the man who tried to kill Duke Thomas and the body of the aircar pilot had one thing in common. Both wore a religious medallion specific to New Earth. The Wyatt took orbit above Keres four hours later and Jilena moved everything to the ship to prevent further attempts on her life on the ground.

Jilena had everyone she felt important in her stateroom plus links to her worlds as Sabella gave a briefing on New Earth.

"New Earth was colonized five hundred and twenty-seven years ago by members of the Protestant Church on Earth. The religion was dying off there and the members of the church sold everything, purchased ship and materials and moved to New Earth. It should be noted that once they had gained a solid foothold on the planet, they did not restrict who moved to the planet and maintained good relationships with various religious groups that moved there."

She paused for a moment.

"The planet prospered until roughly one hundred and sixty-two years ago when they had a planet wide drought which lasted for over two years. Industry suffered due to lack of water and farming nearly became a thing of the past. All of the planet's resources was taken up in staying alive, even with Federation help."

"Then a man named Joshua Canning walked out of the burnt landscape and into Providence, the capital of New Earth, claiming to have had a vision of the future. He began preaching on street corners, atop dry fountains, any place he could get an audience, claiming he could bring the rain back. Some people rejected him as being insane while others, more desperate gave him coinage and fed him as he continued to gather a small, but fanatical following."

Sabella took a sip of water.

"Then the rains returned. It should be noted here that Federation scientists had already pin-pointed when the rains should return as geological records showed periods of drought for the planet approximately every four to five hundred years. By this time Canning was firmly entrenched into the religious society of New Earth and denied the scientific reports of the Federation. His followers believed him and shunned the reports."

"It must be noted that the Federation scientists barely got off the planet alive, with the help of a company of Lancer engineers who had gone in as support of their studies. Within that Lancer unit were several Centaurians."

"Canning began preaching a new path for New Earth and he hit on a couple of economic successes that only grew his popularity. Within a decade he established the Protestant Reformation Church, and his tone changed in doing so. Little by little he changed the position of women until they basically became cattle, servants to the men of the planet."

"He also was preaching that unless a human could trace their heritage back to Mother Earth, then they were not to be trusted, and that creatures such as Centaurians were the Devil's Spawn."

"While he portrayed the part of a vagabond preacher, it was discovered after his death that he was very wealthy, and even had a family. Although it is considered heresy on New Earth to talk about it, it is figured his wife was fourteen when she birthed her first child. And at the time of his death, he had penned a list of prophesies' which several have come true but can be supported by scientific fact if one knew what they were looking for. There is no known vids or photographs of Joshua Canning on record anywhere."

"Based upon what can be determined, New Earth is still under his spell with Canning's grandson now preaching the gospel. Lancer Intelligence has traced millions of credits to members of Congress from small, developing worlds which it is noted have supported, voted for and several have even submitted bills in favor of New Earth. But at this time cannot confirm if the funds were bribes, or loans to those worlds."

"One final note. The goal of the Protestant Reformation Church is to rid the universe of all demons and devils, and to put the universe back on the path of righteousness. They also deny the scientific evidence that the Hayutans were the first humans."

"Thank you, Sabella, that was a fine briefing." Jilena commented. "Now what has the Psych Docs discovered from the two officers they are shredding?"

"Both are full Commanders and have been leading two lives. Even though they are fanatics, they claim to have been given dispensation to fornicate with lesser creatures, meaning Centaurians in order to maintain their cover. As far as the report is concerned, their only instructions from the church was to never allow a report to go beyond them if it had something in it disrespectful to New Earth in it. Disrespectful is a broad term. They disposed of the survey report since you had mentioned the overcharges paid to a New Earth firm and deleted the computer records of it ever having been sent to the Fleet."

"Thank you again Sabella. Duke Thomas, do you have any information or advice?"

Duke Thomas answered from his office on Denoyelles.

"I have nothing new to add to the briefing. Your Yeoman did a superb job in handling it for you. Princess Jilena, I am going to lay this in your lap. How you wish to deal with New Earth is up to you. I can guarantee the Fleet will not interfere as long as it stays in the New Earth Sector. Two members of the Denoyelles family have been targeted for assassination with this last time being twice for you. Evidence shows the failed assassins belonged to the same fanatical group based on New Earth. The Federation has failed in its duty, Your Highness. Take a page from Count Conrad and deal with those who would see you dead."

Thank you, Duke Thomas. Hayuta?"

"Your Highness, the Fleet is standing by awaiting your orders."

"Bellus?"

"Same here Your Highness."

"Zyra?"

"At your command Your Highness."

"Hayuta, transit to Bellus, marry up with their Fleet then on to Zyra to collect theirs. From that point move to the transit point where the two ships are waiting and hold for further orders. My group will proceed directly to New Earth. Your positions are only a day from New Earth and make sure they know you are at the sector border. Execute my orders."

There was a resounding echo of confirmation from Jilena's worlds as she sat and prayed she was doing the right thing. Her tummy was just beginning to swell from the child she carried and if it was born looking like its father, she was not going to see it raised in a universe that declared it a beast.

Ghosts

A day out of Keres, Jilena's group disappeared off all sensors as they transited to New Earth. She assembled her Marines that were aboard the Wyatt and gave them their instructions.

They were to disrupt communications and service utilities without damaging them. How they accomplished that was left up to each individual, but the key was to cause as much panic without actively engaging the people of New Earth. Use the cloaks to appear then disappear quickly giving anyone seeing them the idea they were seeing ghosts. But never let the entire team be seen as the ones still cloaked can watch over the ones exposed. Pilots and crews of the assault boats can do the same with their boats as long as they do not endanger civilians. They were also prohibited from attacking military targets, but if there was some way they could disrupt military training without risk of serious injury, have fun with it.

Upon arrival over New Earth, the Wyatt took a stationary orbit over the capital, Providence, while the other heavy cruisers of her group took orbits equal distances around the planet. A dozen Scout ships took orbits between the cruisers and everyone just waited for Jilena to give the order to drop Marines in their cloaked assault boats.

Jilena had plans within plans for this exercise as she wanted several things to happen. First, she wanted to know exactly where the body of Joshua Canning was interned so a team of Hayutan medical specialists could retrieve it for analysist. As that was happening, she hoped that the disruptions would conceal the first part and cause the New World ruling council into a single location. Hopefully this would also put the current head of their church into that same location.

The first drop was simple. Only one assault boat would drop half of its Marines to run amok and have fun at the citizens expense. From the Wyatt, a second boat went to the surface at the location of Joshua Canning's crypt with the specialists to retrieve his body. As this was happening, all off world communications was blocked, preventing out-going or in-coming communications to be suddenly stopped. This was accomplished by linking a drone to the orbiting communications satellite system and inserting a removable computer worm into the system.

The Marines on the ground were having a field day messing with civilians and authorities. Objects moved about in public in plain view of citizens that should not be moving without assistance. In a crowded restaurant, plates of food moved about tables as people were trying to eat and in one café, a table was suddenly occupied by three Marines who blinked in, then blinked out of view. Reports were being made to local authorities about seeing ghostly images of warriors walking down streets, fully armed for battle then disappearing within seconds of being visible. The Marines were becoming more and more inventive as the public panicked.

Canning's corpse was located in a crypt inside the main church cathedral. Jilena had to laugh at the showmanship the Canning family had undertaken with it as it was in a gas filled case which could be raised behind the church alter for believers to pray to during services. A cloaking device was attached to the glass coffin along with a mag-lifting device to assist in moving it from the cathedral to the assault boat which landed behind the cathedral to take it up to the Wyatt.

Panic ensued when services began being disrupted as water mains were turned down or off, restricting the supply of water to the capital. Electrical services were disconnected at power junctions, leaving power on for hospitals and nursing centers, but leaving the public without power.

Jilena just watched events unfolding on the surface as one team blew up an ammunition bunker near the capital which resulting shock wave broke windows of homes and buildings two kilometers away.

Canning's corpse was well preserved allowing for a clear picture of his face for facial recognition as the medical staff drew DNA samples for testing. They took three samples and ran each sample separately to insure accuracy, then ran the results through the Federation Data Base they were linked to via a back door provided by Duke Thomas.

When the results of the DNA test were confirmed by running two additional searches, Jilena was ready to drop to the capital. Because of her position and her condition with child, special clothing had been made for her that gave her layers of protection, but she could still be injured. Her only complaint about the clothing was that it was heavy and hot, but flexible enough she could still move well enough to use her swords if a fight erupted at close range.

She sent a second set of assault boats to the surface to create further havoc amongst the people as one team watched the council chambers, counting heads and getting visual confirmation that the world's leaders were meeting. Jilena was pleased to hear that Samuel Canning, the current High Priest of the church was in attendance. She dropped with Tamika and Sabella at her side.

Jilena and company entered the council chambers through a side door partially hidden by large curtains and carefully made their way to the stage, avoiding any physical contact with personal or items which might give them away. At the same time, a full section of Marines entered and took positions around the inside of the chambers.

As Jilena was entering the council chambers, two teams were entering the mansion, known as the spiritual retreat of Samuel Canning with an assault boat hovering above it to protect the Marines. Once inside they became visible which created a panic within the harem that Canning had established. Marine

Communication Techs hacked into the computers found in Canning's study and uploaded tera-bites of information to the Wyatt where other techs began to break the information down. It was the harem that disgusted the Marines as several of the 'women' were barely into puberty and one was discovered to be his own sister, impregnated by Canning.

This information was being fed to Jilena as she entered the chambers.

A debate was raging inside the chambers on who was responsible for the failures of civic services and the hysteria of people seeing armed troops within the city that were ghosts in nature. Jilena listened for several minutes before she acted. Jilena's face shield was up and her tiny boom mic in place as she tuned her helmets speakers to fifty percent power before speaking. She was standing off to the left of the Chancellor who was at the podium on the stage when she spoke.

"Silence!" She spoke to the chamber.

This frightened the Chancellor that when he jumped away from the sound of her voice, he tripped and fell. Two council members jumped up to run away to only be pushed back towards their chairs by unseen forces.

"I said silence!"

She spoke again as she dialed up her visibility to the chamber instead of just popping into existence. Jilena only adjusted her cloak to about sixty percent giving her a shimmering effect as if there yet not there. This was almost as startling as her voice out of nowhere.

"I am Jilena, the Throne of Hayuta and Bellus, Protector of Keres and Hawkings World. I've came for the one who ordered my death, and the death of Duke Thomas Denoyelles. Give him to me or all of you will suffer my wrath."

135

One man bolted for the door but ran into an armored Marine causing the man to stagger back, dazed before he was spun around and pushed back to where he had been sitting.

Jilena pointed to the Chancellor who was still on the floor.

"Who ordered my death? Speak before I remove your manhood and sell you to Raiders for their pleasure!"

"He did! He ordered your death to protect the church!" Was the reply she received from the Chancellor.

"Who is he? Tell me now!" Jilena was playing the part of a vengeful wraith.

"The High Priest, Lord Canning! Samuel Canning!"

Jilena turned her attention to the chamber.

"Bring Canning to me!" She ordered.

No one moved but a voice was heard.

"You're a woman! You have not authority here!"

Jilena laughed.

"Yes, in violation of Federation Articles, you have taken away the rights of your women. Turned them into property, instead of partners or mates. Bring Canning to me, now!"

The man who had earlier tried to make a break from the chambers stood and pointed at Jilena.

"You're a witch, a whore who has bred with the beast. You have no power in this holy place!"

Again, Jilena laughed.

"You must be Canning. Would you care to meet my husband, the one you call a beast?"

"I have no fear of the beast as I have the Almighty at my side!"

That was what Tamika was waiting for as he suddenly popped into full view as Jilena turned her cloak to full exposure. The panic would have been complete if not for all of the Marines in the chamber popping into view. The council members quickly recognized they were trapped.

"Bring him to me." Tamika ordered.

Two Marines grabbed the man they already knew to be Samuel Canning and drug him to the stage as the rest of the council cowered in their chairs. His efforts to resist failed as he did not have the strength to combat to Hayutan Marines. They positioned him in front of Tamika, then stepped aside. Tamika reached over his shoulder and slowly pulled his long sword from its sheath as he grinned at Canning. Canning urinated on himself.

Instead of striking Canning with his sword, Tamika drove in into the podium, cutting a large chunk of wood and metal from it, then pointing the sword at Canning.

"For ordering the death of my bride, and my unborn child, I should take my time and remove pieces of your body until your own mother would not recognize you."

Canning fainted.

Jilena burst out in laughter.

"My husband, I do not think his faith in his Almighty was as strong as he let on. Marines, remove this filth and ready him for transport to the iron mines of Denoyelles."

She waited until the Marines had removed Canning from the chambers.

"Council of New Earth, I give you a choice. Correct your mistakes from living under a Theocracy. Your Canning was a false prophet as was his father and grandfather. Look to the space above your world and you will see I have placed a Fleet around your world as you slept. My Marines walk your streets, hidden as they were hidden inside these chambers. You know of the Fleet at the edge of the sector and be it known that the Federation Fleet cannot and will not protect you if I decide to turn this world into a burned-out cinder."

She paused in hope what she was saying was getting through to these men.

"I do not care why this council was determined to undermine the Articles of the Federation, or what you attempted to gain from it. The violations we have uncovered is worthy of taking each of your heads, but I give you this one chance to redeem yourselves. Until you can prove that you function in the Federation under Federation Articles, your off-world accounts are frozen, your Embassy's will be closed, and the Embassy's here on New Earth will be emptied, isolating you from the rest of the Federation."

"You must prove to the Throne of Bellus and Hayuta that you are worthy of being a member of the Federation. And you have five years to prove this before nature once more places this world into a drought such as the one that gave you Joshua Canning, who we know as Reginald Robateau from Hawkings World, who was a brilliant student and scientist until he was tried and convicted for pedophilia before he escaped custody. It does not matter to the Throne if you believe the truth about your Canning, but he conned you and used you for his own means as he taught his way of life to his son and grandson."

"Go to Canning's sanctuary and you may find those young girls that are missing there, used for his sexual pleasure while preaching modesty."

Jilena drew her long sword and held it up in front of her.

138

"I am Princess Jilena, the Throne of Bellus and Hayuta, Protector of Keres and Zyra. What I have spoken to you is verifiable and my promise to you is my bond. Do not test me further than you have."

With that she blinked out along with all of her Marines, Tamika and Sabella who was recording all that was said and occurred in the chambers.

As Jilena was speaking to the Council, Comm Techs had broken into the New Earth Government computers and had downloaded them to a computer storage unit in Cargo Bay Four of the Wyatt. They also installed a worm which would continue sending data to a site on Keres for further examination with each entry into the computer by government officials.

Revelations

When the Wyatt boosted from orbit around New Earth, Jilena took the entire cloaked group with her and replaced them with the ships that had sat at the edge of the sector, except for ten medium Hayutan cruisers which had cloaking capability which she added to her group.

What would have been a six-day transit for the Wyatt, became eight as Jilena's Scout Ships were not as fast as her heavy cruiser, as Jilena was heading for Hanover and the Federation Capital. But this also gave Jilena's techs time to rip the data apart from Canning's and the New Earth Government's computers apart to see how deep the corruption within the Federation had spread.

The Wyatt was crowded with additional personal working in Cargo Bay Four, sorting through volumes of information, connecting New Earth to corrupt politicians at the Federation Capital. As each politician was confirmed by payoffs notated in the stolen computer data, that information was sent to Duke Thomas, who in turn insured that the Admiral of the Fleet had the information. The Hanover Worlds System was locked down, with the Fleet not allowing any ship to transit from the system.

Two days out of Hanover, Duke Thomas contacted Jilena on their secure link.

"Princess, were you considering entering the system concealed?"

"It is a thought Lord Duke."

"Come in concealed and send a shuttle for me. We need to talk, face to face, before you go to Hanover."

"As you wish Lord Duke. Is there something we need to know?"

"You'll know everything once we meet. Safe journey, Princess."

Jilena just sat back in her chair once the conversation with Duke Thomas was disconnected thinking she had enough on her mind, now he is wanting to meet. She decided that since she had no control over why the Duke wished to meet, she would be better off using her energies in preparing to meet the Federation Congress.

She took comfort that the Admiral of the Fleet was arranging for Fleet personal who might go against his orders to stand away from the confrontation between the Thrones and the Federation Congress to be isolated, placed in positions where they could do no harm.

Reports from Hayutan agents already on Hanover told of mass confusion within the Embassy's aligned with New Earth and their inability to contact that world, receiving only static in return.

Jilena was playing a high stakes game with the worlds she had sworn to protect, but it was a game that had to be played, much as Count Conrad played to liberate the Hanover Worlds.

She had Tamika handle the tactical side of dispersing her Fleet upon entering the Hanover System, knowing that her gathering of ships could not properly cover the three worlds of the system, but being cloaked, concealed, gave her Fleet the advantage. Jilena stood beside Tamika in Combat as they entered the system watching as her Fleet dispersed to their assigned positions.

Once in orbit, a cloaked assault boat was sent to pick up Duke Thomas at his estate on Denoyelles. When the Duke exited the boat, he was given full honors on the hanger deck with two platoons of Marines making a corridor for him to pass through to Jilena, Tamika, and the rest of her staff and ship's officers.

The Duke carried a large scroll and behind him, his military aide carried a sheathed sword in both hands. The Duke stopped within a meter of Jilena and bowed his head as Jilena returned the courtesy. Jilena thought he looked exceptional for a man approaching eighty. Jilena spoke first.

"Lord Thomas Crandall, Duke Denoyelles, we are honored to have you aboard my flagship, the Cruiser Wyatt."

"Thank you Princess Jilena for such honors as your Marines are well turned out. I am pleased to see such warriors, and in their presences, I have something important to say as they can all witness this occasion."

"What might that be Duke Thomas?"

"Your Royal Highness, Princess Jilena, I have come to you today to transfer the right to the Hanover Throne to you as I am retiring from public service."

He handed the scroll to Jilena.

"Contained within this scroll is the lineage of the Denoyelles family and your place in it. As of this moment, you are now the Duchess Denoyelles, heir to the Throne of Hanover."

Jilena was speechless as she accepted the scroll. Lord Thomas then turned to his aide and took the sword from him with both hands and turned back to Jilena, holding it in front of him in both hands.

"Your Royal Highness, this is Count Conrad Denoyelles sword. With this sword comes the right to ascend to the Throne of Hanover, if you so desire and feel the need. Please accept this burden from me as it is a heavy burden to carry and I no longer feel capable of bearing such a burden."

Jilena handed the scroll to Tamika, then stepped forward to Lord Thomas, took one knee and accepted the sword.

"Lord Thomas, I do not feel worthy of such an honor, but I will strive to insure the Denoyelles name is never tarnished as long as I have a breath of air in my lungs."

"Then rise Duchess Denoyelles, there is much to do, and time is short. Rebellion is in the air this day, and it must be contained before war spreads across the known universe."

As Jilena rose a cry came from the ranks.

"Long live the Duchess!"

The cheer was taken up by all hands present and echoed within the hanger bay. Jilena motioned to Lord Thomas to follow as she turned and left the hanger bay for her stateroom with the cheers following behind her. She did not speak until they were in her stateroom.

"Lord Thomas, why are you doing this now?"

"Princess, to be honest I am afraid I may have feet of clay in reference to what needs to be dealt with over the next days and weeks. I was raised to business, but this calls for a warrior, something I was never good at, and not trained for. With your permission I shall continue to manage the family's business until you can be completely brought into it, but beyond that, I would be a weak link in a strong chain. A chain which needs to bind the universe back together or all of the work our ancestor did was for naught."

"Lord Thomas, you shall always be welcome in my house, and forever be thought of as the Duke of Denoyelles. Please stay and advise me, because I need voices to give me caution, to insure I do not burn down the universe as I try to save it."

"You have good advisors already My Princess, but I will attend as an advisor where I can."

"Good, now within my stateroom, in the privacy of my house, please, Jilena is all I need to be known as."

143

Lord Thomas laughed.

"You were properly named. Count Conrad's precious Jilena was also that way according to the writings of the Count. Now, there are plans to be made and as I said, time is short. The Congress will meet in less than three hours, and it is becoming divided as we speak. It is an uneven division as those worlds who have been hurt by the laws and tariffs passed are gathering to rebel against those rulings, even if it means war."

"The Fleet? How does it stand?"

"It stands with the Articles they were sworn to support and defend. A handful of officers have sided with the corruption, but that is mostly honoring their worlds, not the corruption itself. If you take the Throne, the Fleet is yours to command."

"I do not want the Throne, Lord Thomas."

"Jilena My Love, it might be wise to take the Throne." Tamika spoke up.

"Why is that Tamika?"

"It is the one place that the corruption has not touched. It is also a neutral position, detached from the Federation Congress. From the Throne, you can guide with a firm hand, instead of a blade."

"Duke Tamika is right, My Lady." Lord Thomas commented.

"Duke Tamika? Tamika questioned.

"Most certainly, Duke Tamika. A Duchess needs a Duke does she not? And you are properly wedded, bonded, so function follows form."

Tamika looked at Jilena.

"You know, I was a simple Lancer Captain when I met you. Now look at me, first a Prince, now a Duke, and it's all your fault woman!" He was smiling as he spoke.

"Yes, well this demon spawn growing inside me is your fault, so we're even." Jilena rose up and gave him a quick peck on his lips.

"Now, where were we?" Jilena brought the conversation back to reality.

They worked on how to gain the attention of the Council and Congress for over an hour. Every plan had its problems and its advantages. The problem was how deep the corruption had infected the Government, having everyone in the Chambers of Congress meant they could have them contained. Lord Thomas still had control of the Second Lancer Regiment and ordered them to not only secure the Capital grounds, but to insure no one entered the Chambers with any manner of arms, even ceremonial daggers.

Jilena ordered her Marines into her Royal Livery in preparation for deploying them into the Capital. She tried to eat before going to the surface but all she did was pick at the fruit on her plate.

"What's wrong My Love?" Tamika asked.

"Tamika, this is nothing like ascending to a Throne. We have one group of mostly neutral worlds waiting for the blade to fall. Another group that is openly talking rebellion against the tariffs placed upon them by the third group which has bribed their way past the Articles of Federation. If I take a misstep, then we could see the start of a planetary war which no one wants."

"Jilena, listen to me. The war has already started, it's just that no one is shooting yet. Hopefully you can cause all of the participants to step back and take a breath before the shooting starts. I would be willing to bet that everyone that will be in those Chambers today are afraid of a war, even if they are the ones who would start it. Give them a greater fear to consider. The fear of having to deal with you instead of with each other."

"I'm not sure I have the strength."

"Princess." Lord Thomas entered the conversation. "Much like when fate placed you in front of that Liger, fate has once again has placed you in grave danger. Only this time you are not alone with just a sword to deal with the threat, you have trusted ones beside you, a Fleet greater than anything Count Conrad had at his fingertips, and you have the Articles of Federation to support your decisions. It took the Count months to dig out the information you have at hand concerning where the corruption is deepest. Root that out and set the Federation of Worlds back on its original path."

"You make it seem so simple Lord Thomas." Jilena responded to his comments.

"My Lady, if it was that simple, I could have done it myself, but it will take the inner strength you have to make this happen."

Jilena was quiet as she slowly ate, thinking about what was said and trying to overcome the doubt in her mind. Fear and anger had driven her earlier decisions, fear of losing those most precious to her and the anger that people were willing to kill hundreds, even thousands to see her dead. Now those feelings were past, and she was left alone with the uncertainty of her actions.

The clock was running against her, and she had come too far in such a short time to turn back.

The Throne of Hanover

Jilena's cloaked assault boat landed on the Green behind the former Palace of Hanover. The Green where the Blade of Justice still stood since long before Count Conrad, ready to remove the heads of those whose crimes demanded such punishment.

Three boats had already landed, packed full of her Hayutan Marines dressed in her Royal Livery in preparation of securing the Palace and the connected Federation Chambers. Behind her three more boats waited their turn to land and discharge their cargo of Marines.

Jilena decloaked as she entered the Palace to be greeted by a Lancer Captain who had earlier secured the Palace on Lord Thomas's orders. He never spoke of her cloaking ability and just guided her to the Throne Room of the Palace.

At one time the Throne of Hanover set on a meter-high platform, so the old Counts could look out over his subjects, but Count Conrad had changed that. Now there was a large, circular table with an ornate, yet modest chair which Conrad had declared as the Throne. Jilena walked up to that chair, knowing she would have to occupy it, even if she had no desire to sit in it.

She looked down at the floor in front of the chair and envisioned the blood spilled by the wound received by the original Jilena, who as Count Conrad's concubine, had thrown her body across Conrad's to protect him from being shot by one of the Dukes who sat around the table during their meetings.

Jilena smiled at the thought that if the original Jilena, who was nothing more than a member of Conrad's harem could place herself in harm's way to protect the man she loved, then she could find the strength to do what had to be done this day.

She stood remembering that Conrad hated the concubine system and only took Jilena into his on a bluff that failed, forcing him to make her his concubine, then later his lover. The three women who the people of Hanover thought were his concubines, were actually Centaurian Lancers contracted to protect him, even though they also became his lovers during that time. Jilena laughed out loud how things seemed to come full circle. She too had a Centaurian lover who was there to protect her.

"Your Highness, the Congress is complete with all members present except for Lord Thomas." The Lancer Captain spoke from behind her.

"Then it's time. Tamika, order the Royal Guard to decloak and enter the Chamber as planned. Captain, take us to the Chamber please." Jilena instructed.

The Federation President was standing at the podium, trying to gain some order when the doors to the Chamber opened and Hayutan Marines entered wearing Jilena's Royal livery. Protests rang out from the members of Congress as the President looked left and right to see his avenues of escape were blocked by Royal Guards.

Less than two minutes later, Jilena entered with Tamika, Lord Thomas, and Sabella following.

"What is the meaning of this Princess Jilena?" The President questioned.

"The meaning of this Lord Eschmann is that I have come to correct a wrong. Lord Eschmann, you are under arrest for treason under the Article of the Federation. Guards, secure Lord Eschmann."

Two Royal Guards moved to Eschmann, took him by the arms and pulled him away from the podium as he protested the actions.

"Guards, if he does not shut his mouth, shut it for him." She ordered. This cause Eschmann to become silent as Jilena moved to the podium.

"Lords and Ladies, members of the Federation Council and Congress. My words are being broadcasted across the Federation as I speak them, so all worlds will know why I am here today."

There was a chorus of protests from the floor of Congress demanding her to remove herself as she just stood looking out over the Chambers. She pulled her short sword and hammered the butt of the handle on the podium, silencing the protests. Jilena laid the sword across the podium before continuing to speak.

"Let me start with this. If those of you are wondering why there is no contact with New Earth, it is simple. A portion of my Fleet is in space above New Earth blocking all communications and travel into and from New Earth. I moved on New Earth because of evidence the attempts on my life and the life of Duke Thomas originated from there. We now have further evidence of that fact plus evidence of corruption within the Federation Congress in violation of the Article of Federation. Corruption which has placed the Federation on the edge of war. Rebellion by worlds who were being punished for no other reason than greed. Greed for money and power."

She paused before continuing.

"We have the records of the one called Simon Canning, the so called High Priest of New Earth, showing bribes paid to members of Congress, to include the President to enact laws which gave one planet power over another in violation of the Articles."

"We have records showing the sale of young girls from New Earth and several other worlds into prostitution and those girls being used by members of Congress before and after the sale. Girls corrupted by Simon Canning for his own deviant pleasure.

149

Girls so young, many had not even reached the age to have their first cycle."

"Before any one present begins to complain about under what authority I have to disrupt this Congress and arrest the President and others today, I shall explain in simple terms."

"Earlier today Duke Thomas, the Duke Denoyelles, retired, naming me as heir to the Denoyelles chair and to the Throne of Hanover. I, Jilena Kaylani Borland Gannaway, Princess Jilena who sits on the Thrones of Hayuta and Bellus, sworn Protector of Keres and Hawkings World, do hereby claim my right to ascend to the Throne of Hanover. I claim this right because the Congress has corrupted all that my ancestor Count Conrad had worked to prevent, so it is my duty to set things back right. I command the Federation Fleet, I command the Lancers, and I have the Fleets of five systems to support them."

"I will not tolerate rebellion within the Federation!" Her words were shape.

"Worlds that have a grievance with the current laws of the Federation, need only to petition the Throne for relief. To the worlds that have either willingly or unknowingly been a part of this infestation of corruption, the Throne gives you the leeway to present your case before the Throne. As the Throne, I do hereby swear that the people, the families of all worlds shall not suffer because of the greed and corruption of their leaders. Remove them if you can, if you cannot, my Fleet will come and take care of that for you."

"There will be no war, no rebellion. To the Worlds of the Federation I also caution that civil war on a world will not be tolerated or I shall send my Lancers to quell such a thing. The evidence we have garnered will be provided to each world and with that evidence, you can remove your leaders to stand trial. This includes the leaders of industry who worked to bribe civic leaders to benefit from the corruption.

"These are my words, and my word is my bond, for I am Princess Jilena, the Throne of Hanover."

As she was leaving the podium, her Royal Guards moved to arrest those that had already been named in the documents from New Earth. Soon the Federation Communications Center was overwhelmed with calls and messages for the Throne. Jilena went to Count Conrad's former apartment and waited for the chaos to calm down.

Tamika sent a message from the Center to all worlds under her name that told the people of the worlds that the Throne would prosecute any individuals who violated the rights of those named in the corruption. By the Articles, they had a right to a trial and that right would not be wavered.

Turmoil then Calm

Jilena sat in Conrad's office apartment reading through stacks of messages from all over the Federation, with some reporting on events on that world in removing the corruption or requests for help.

Lancer assault carriers were lifting hourly as she dispatched companies or battalions to worlds requesting help in removing leaders that were hiding behind private armies. Her Fleets were busy intercepting those that had escaped their worlds only to find they had no place to run to in their attempt to escape justice.

A week after Jilena ascended to the Hanover Throne she once again went before the vid cameras to speak to the people of the Federation. She sat in Count Conrad's office, wearing a pewter grey suit as she spoke to the Federation.

"Citizens of the Federation, I, Jilena, come to you today to answer questions about my ascension to the Hanover Throne. There are rumors that I intend to impose a dictatorship over the Federation Worlds. Those rumors are false. The actions I took last week was to preserve the Federation, to prevent rebellion. The last time a Denoyelles forced their will on the Federation, it was because it was as corrupt as it is now, and Count Conrad withdrew from the Federation only to find himself President of a newly formed Federation here on Hanover."

"The Articles of Federation which Count Conrad wrote were designed for all people, regardless of sex, age, racial background, social standing, wealth to be equal before the law with no individual, group, or planet superior to another. Those Articles were corrupted by people who wished for power over others. Their touch was so soft for a long time that no one noticed the loss of freedoms until they became almost unbearable to carry."

"As the Hayutan Council and the Council of Bellus can attest, I have no desire to rule over any people or worlds, but I carry the Denoyelles blood and cannot ignore the legacy of that blood."

"I did not accept the Hayutan Throne because I desired power. I went before the Hayutan Council with full intent to renounce the throne, but was convinced to accept it not by family, who supported my not taking the throne, not by the Hayutan Council who wanted me on the throne, but by a scholar whom I had heard teach against Royal leadership at the university on Bellus."

"That scholar begged me to take the throne and humbled himself before me. I heard his plea and ascended the throne. Then when Bellus asked me to take the Throne of Bellus, once again another asked me to accept. This time is was a legendary Lancer who came to me when I was undecided and convinced me to accept the Throne of Bellus."

"It should be known to the Worlds of the Federation that neither individual asked for favor or gratitude. One even offered their neck for being impertinent."

"Hawkings World, or Zyra, the Hayutan name for the world came to me on Bellus and asked for my Protection as the Thorne of Hayuta and Bellus. We must remember that Hawkings World was the first world discovered that had been settled then abandoned by the early Hayutans. These worlds were connected in ways we could not understand until my Grandmother, Princess Lujayn was kidnapped and taken to Hayuta to become their first Royal in decades. Once Princess Lujayn took the Hayutan Throne is was discovered that Keres was also part of the Hayutan Worlds."

"Lord Mikhail LaSalle, Lord Protector of Keres retired and as his Great-Granddaughter, he appointed me to be the new Protector of Keres, so he could retire."

"By my taking the Hanover Throne, the circle is complete as Mother Earth was the first of the Hayutan Worlds to be seeded and used as an experiment. An experiment that far exceeded the expectations of the early Hayutans."

"As I stated earlier, I do not, did not want to sit on the thrones of any of these worlds, but the corruption that has been eating at the Federation forced me to do this for the citizens who had no voice. Citizens who would suffer if their leaders set their worlds on the path of rebellion."

"Now to confirm one rumor. Yes, the Hayutans have a cloak which hides their ships and even individuals. They have been in space eons before mankind sailed the oceans of Mother Earth. They used these cloaks as they watched humanity move out into the universe."

"Princess Lujayn had all cloaking devices removed from Hayutan vessels when she took the Throne, and forbid the use of any type cloak once Hayuta entered the Federation. But with the rumor of rebellion, these devices were not only brought out of retirement, they have been improved on, making them safer from being captured and used by Raiders or Slavers."

"This now brings me to something vital to the peace of the Federation. As soon as practical, I am sending Fleets into the uncharted areas to search for the camps of Raiders and Slavers. I intend to find them and remove them from our speech. If we cannot find them it is because we are driving them so deep into uncharted space that it will be unprofitable for them to continue their activities."

"Citizens of the Federation I ask that you help me in maintaining calm while the Federation rebuilds itself in the vision which Count Conrad Denoyelles once envisioned where each individual, each world is equal to the next. Where an individual born in poverty has the chance to improve his condition through honest study and labor."

"I, Princess Jilena, ask the citizens of the Federation to remain calm during this time of confusion as we work to correct the wrongs placed upon all of us by corrupt officials for their personal gain."

"I thank you for your time and may the Saints watch over us."

What Jilena had not said was that the Hayutans had fielded a new generation of Scout Ships, the Atlas Class which was twenty percent larger than the previous Gemini Class with better armor, fifty percent faster and better weapon systems. Thirty of those vessels were already in uncharted space watching four worlds where either Raiders or Slavers were operating from. Jilena had decided to send them out on that mission instead of acting as part of her group during the move on New Earth as she used the Gemini Class Scout ships.

Their mission was to watch and track any vessels leaving those worlds in hopes to locate other Outlaw bases. Within hours of Jilena's speech, ships lifted from those bases, guiding Scouts to other bases deep within uncharted space. The Scout ships begin landing, off-loading their Marine Support Crews to recon the bases and determine nature.

Slaver bases were the first moved on, with cloaked Hayutan Frigates moving on them, blocking all communications from the planets as they dropped their Marine companies to the surface to free the slaves from their bondage. The fact that the Marines were cloaked as they raided these bases not only prevented deaths amongst the Marines during the assault on the bases but helped prevent the slavers from killing the slaves as had happened in earlier attempts by Federation forces.

It would be four months into this operation before Jilena allowed this news to be broadcast to the worlds of the Federation.

A New Home

It was unknown to the worlds of the Federation that there was a prison for people like Samuel Canning. People who short of being lobotomized could never reenter society. Near the North Pole of the ice-covered planet Sukowa, in the Hanover System, was a prison of sorts for people like Canning.

With the average temperature being minus twenty-five centigrade, there was no need for fences or walls around this prison. Life outside the massive buildings of the prison was measured in seconds as no human could survive the bitter cold without protective clothing. And the doors exiting out into the frigid wasteland around the prison were not guarded nor locked.

No guards walked the corridors of the prison allowing the prisoners to deal with each other as they wished. Samuel Canning was castrated by order of Princess Jilena and sent to this frozen hell as his sentence for his perversions. He was raped three times the first day by other inmates. Jilena had not had him lobotomized so he would understand each perversion against his body.

Eighteen days after entering the prison, Samuel Canning took a walk outside. No one attempted to collect his sexually abuse body.

Jilena was in her fourth month of pregnancy when she appointed her elder brother, Alton, as her Lord Secretary to Hanover. Her new palace on Keres was complete and she wanted to get away from Hanover and the daily business of the Federation. It wasn't so much the business of the Federation she was getting away from as it was the constant pleas for an audience for what she considered trivial matters, matters that to her should be dealt with at the Minister or Ambassador level.

By the time she landed outside her new home on Keres, all of the trials of the corrupted officials had been completed. Most knowing the evidence was solidly against them pleaded guilty and were sent to the iron mines on Denoyelles with sentences ranging from ten years to life. Two were sent to Sukowa to spend their days viewing the frozen world around them.

It was revealed during the trials and the Psych interrogation of Samuel Canning that the people behind the corruption was hoping that by killing Jilena, then Duke Thomas, another would become the Denoyelles Chair and be agreeable to bribes, even though the Denoyelles family was the wealthiest family in the Universe. Wealthier than most worlds within the Federation.

The trials on New Earth took a different turn as Jilena gave permission for the parents of the stolen children the right to determine punishment if it was proven any official had used any of the young girls. One official was taken out into the wilderness and stabbed in the stomach by the father of one girl and left to die alone from his wound. Most were hung in the town square of the Capital as a warning to others.

Federation Marines walked the streets of Providence, the Capital insuring peace as women regained their rights and freedoms, often at the painful expense of their spouses who had abused them believing it was their right to treat them as servants. Divorce was simple in that the women tossed those men out with nothing and the Federation tribunal overseeing the change on New Earth gave all rights to property and children to the women, with very few exceptions.

Jilena was in her new home less than a week when she wrote a proposal to her worlds concerning the heir to the Thrones. She stated that the silver hair was proven to be a genetic adaptation by the Hayutans to prove heritage and with DNA research as advanced as it currently was, the hair no longer mattered. The DNA had been altered in a single blood line so on the worlds where the Hayutans were experimenting with the humans they had transplanted there a lineage would be simple in determining who sat on the Throne.

She proposed that since the Hanover Throne was determined by blood, not by the silver of one's hair, all the worlds should follow suit. Jilena left it up to the people themselves, the citizens of her worlds to vote for her proposal. She noted that the birth of a child with silver hair had skipped several generations, leaving the Thrones unattended.

The citizens of Hayuta, Bellus, Zyra, and Keres all confirmed her proposal meaning that Jilena's first born would be in line to ascend the Thrones, regardless of the color of their hair.

Jilena was in her seventh month when she had to return to Hanover to seat the new Federation Government as new planetary governments had been rebuilt from the corrupt ones and new Ambassadors appointed to sit in Congress.

She sat before Congress as her swollen belly made it hard for her to stand very long and gave the new Congress the Principals of Leadership as written by her Grandmother.

Jilena was strong in her wording of what would happen if those Principals were violated by any member of Congress. Except for New Earth, no member of the previous Congress had been executed for their corruption, but to violate the Principals of Leadership for personal gain would earn that individual a trip to the Green and be introduced to the Blade.

Congress went to work removing laws, rulings, regulations and tariffs that had hindered the growth of developing planets. Aid packages were voted on where needed with a reminder that the aid was to assist in moving the worlds forward, not to maintain them. Each world had to make their own way in the universe, not be hand carried through aid packages.

Taxes on the citizens, corporations, and worlds was restricted to one percent of annual income. The only deduction for charity that could be taken was for donations to the Hanover

Foundation which Count Conrad had started and still did valuable work within the Federation.

Jilena warned the Directors of the Hanover Foundation to maintain the rules they had first been formed under and to remember that Count Conrad established the Foundation to assist his citizens in rising above their conditions, not to support those conditions.

As she returned to Keres, Jilena fought the urge to step down from the Throne, but knew that to do so would allow some to try to circumvent her plans for a new Federation. But the plans were not truly hers, as they were the ideas her Grandmother had set into motion with the Principals of Leadership.

As Count Conrad had developed his Articles upon the Principals of Command he worked under as a Lancer, Princess Lujayn had refined them using the Fleet's Command Guidance Handbook, adapting those principals to a civilian society.

Jilena christened her long-time assistant, Sabella, Lady Sabella upon returning home as a reward for her service and made her the Lady Secretary to Keres. Sabella then married her lover, Jilena's cousin, Corbin Devore in a ceremony at the new Palace.

Life around the Palace for Jilena was much calmer than on Hanover as her small staff tried to insure she rested as her pregnancy progressed. Especially during the last month of her pregnancy when her Altairian doctor ordered her to bed because of the stress she was dealing with.

The first onset of labor began in the middle of the night for Jilena and sixteen hours later she gave birth to a son who she named Ismael Alexander. Ismael was born with coal black hair as his father, but without the fur of a Centaurian.

Celebrations were held all over the Federation upon hearing of the birth of an heir to what was becoming known as the Hayutan Worlds.

A Lasting Peace?

Ismael was two when the campaign against the Raiders and slavers finally came to an end. The Fleet could not determine if they had totally wiped each group out, but there had been no attacks for over a year and as the Fleet pushed further into uncharted space, looking for the bases of those people finding less and less as time progressed.

Jilena traveled to New Earth just after Ismael turned three to meet with that world's new government and to welcome them back into the Federation. Shortly after her return to Keres, she learned she was once again pregnant. She would give birth to another son, again free of the Centaurian coat of fur, but with her red hair. She named him Thomas Conrad after Lord Thomas and Count Conrad.

There is no such creature as peace, as defined by scholars, but the peace that finally settled over the Federation was one which Jilena did not have to act upon as she raised her sons.

Ismael was ten when Jilena learned she was pregnant again and in her fifth month, Tamika had himself fixed so this would be their last. This time they had a daughter who like her father was covered in a fine coat of fur but was a light brown covering. Tamika named her Pilar Lujayn.

Human nature being as it is would not allow true peace to reign over the Federation. Civil wars erupted on worlds where the people found themselves in conflict, often with the Principals of Leadership. Anarchists rose and fell, trying to change the structure of life on their world. Groups who demanded the Government provide all their needs without being able to explain how to generate the funding to provide that need. Other Groups demanding strict compliance to the Principals as they interrupted them in a strict sense, without any measure of leeway.

Before her passing, Princess Lujayn wrote several treatises on the Principals of Leadership dealing with their meanings and her intentions when she wrote them. Jilena wrote several opinions to Lujayn's treatises, further explaining them but as since the time before humanity moved into space, no matter how well the explanations were written, someone either ignored them or tried to further interpret them to suit their own visions.

Lord Popkyn passed after thirty years of serving as Lord Secretary to Hayuta. Although it was known he had taken lovers in the early years of his posting to Hayuta, he never married or bonded with one of his lovers.

Jilena appointed her younger half-sister, Lucy, by her step-mother Johanne, as her Secretary to Hayuta. When they cleaned out Popkyn's quarter's they discovered a locked box. Once opened it only contained a sealed, thick envelope with Jilena's name on it. Lucy hand carried the envelope to Jilena on Keres.

The Bellus Prophecy

Inside the envelope were Popkyn's notes on his research of the Golden Tablet to include photographs of the tablet from several different angles. Along with the notes was another smaller, sealed envelope. In it was a rubbing of the tablet where a piece of paper had been laid over the tablet and then rubbed to transfer the symbols to the paper.

But the accompanying paper to it was a complete interpretation of the tablet. This was the secret Popkyn could not tell her.

At the top of the second page was a reference to an ancient language belonging to the aborigines people of North America on Mother Earth. The note stated the language was the written language of the Cherokee People. She read Popkyn's interpretation.

"The peace of the universe is disrupted by people who wished for power above all others. From the original people, not of Earth, will come one to return the universe to peace. She will come with hair of fire and silver and right the wrongs of the universe. She will marry one whose fur coat is as black as night, and they shall reign over peace as their children will follow in their foot prints."

The only information concerning the tablet that could be confirmed was that it was over a thousand years old. Jilena folded the page back up and returned it to its envelope and resealed it. The entire package was resealed without any other person reading the message.

Tamika asked her what the message said and Jilena told him to rest easy as it was right that Popkyn hid it from her. If she had known of this prophecy, would she had taken the path she had walked?

When it was announced a new class of Frigate would come out of the Denoyelles shipyards, Jilena ordered the class to be referred to as the Popkyn Class with the first ship to be named after Lord Popkyn.

Jilena sat on the Throne of the Federation as it was now called until her seventy-fifth birthday when she turned over the Throne to Ismael. She moved into the small retreat with Tamika where they had first made love and each evening watched the sun set knowing they had lived a good life, and still had a lot of life left to live together.

About the Author

Leon Michaels is the author of several novels and short stories that reflect his twenty-three years of military service. Michaels enlisted in the Marine Corps in 1970 and has memberships in the Veterans of Foreign Wars, the American Legion, the Disabled American Veterans organizations, NRA, and Rotary International. In 1971, he married his high school sweetheart, raised three daughters and has three grandsons. He calls Creek County, Oklahoma home.

Made in the USA
Columbia, SC
20 February 2018